Life Without Water

Life Without Water

a novel

BY NANCY PEACOCK

LONGSTREET PRESS
ATLANTA, GEORGIA

Published by
LONGSTREET PRESS, INC.
A subsidiary of Cox Newspapers,
A subsidiary of Cox Enterprises, Inc.
2140 Newmarket Parkway
Suite 118
Marietta, GA 30067

Printed in the United States of America

2nd printing 1996

Library of Congress Catalog Card Number: 96-76501

ISBN: 1-56352-337-X

Jacket and book design by Paulette Livers Lambert
Typesetting by Jill Dible

An earlier, condensed version of *Life Without Water* originally appeared in The St. Andrews Review.

"Feel Like I'm Fixin' to Die Rag" copyright © 1965, renewed 1993 Alkatraz Corner Music
Company. Words and music by Joe McDonald. Used by permission.

IN MEMORY OF CARRIE REED

I would like to thank the following people for their help and support: Lee Smith, Janet Hurley, Marjorie Hudson, Tony Peacock, Patricia Mickelberry, and Amanda Monath.

Life Without Water

' pivotal point in your life.

C H A P T E R   O N E

My name is Cedar and I was born in 1969 in one bedroom of a gray and tumbling house in Chatham County, North Carolina. My mother's name is Sara. My father called himself Sol. My mother has told me over and over and over again the story of their courtship, the story of my birth and her reasons for being with this man called Sol. My mother has told me that if not for her brother Jimmie's death, I might not have ever been born. She thinks she might not have found my father so fascinating if Jimmie had only lived. She thinks her whole life has pivoted on that moment, long before I was conceived, before my mother had even met my father, that moment in 1968, when she was home for spring break, visiting her parents in Atlanta, Georgia, and the doorbell rang.

She opened the wide white door to her parents home and found a crisp military man standing there. It was late morning. She was just getting up. Behind the house she could hear the drone of the lawn mower as her father cut across the grass. From the kitchen her mother sang out, "Who is it, dear?"

My mother says that she knew immediately who it was. Without the man saying a word, she knew that six weeks before his tour was up, Jimmie was dead and that he had died in the mud and jungles of Vietnam and that his buttons and shoes were never as polished as this man's were.

My Uncle Jimmie was survived by my mother, Sara, and by their parents and that was all.

My Uncle Jimmie was walking point and he stepped on a mine and was blown to bits. This is what my mother says. These are her exact words and after she says them she repeats, "To bits," always shaking her head. There was no body. Only an empty casket made of dark, gleaming wood. Wood so bright that, during the funeral, the sun reflected off of it and shone like a block into my mother's eyes.

Momma has remembered out loud to me the coldness of the metal chairs they sat on, the sight of the fat triangle of flag being presented to her mother, the smell of freshly dug ground in April. "It smelled like a garden," Momma always says at this point. "Just like spring." She looks down and almost whispers to me the story of the bluebird that landed on the pile of raw earth and how it lifted its head in song and beside my mother, my grandmother burst into tears and pressed her face into the flag.

My Uncle Jimmie died six weeks before his tour would have been up. In just six short weeks he might have been home, his feet propped up on the coffee table. He might have visited my mother at school and smoked a joint with her and told her about the killer dope in Vietnam. He might have defended the war. He might not have. I might not have ever been born.

My uncle sent my mother a necklace which he had made by drilling a hole through a bullet and threading it with a leather thong. My mother had decided to send it back.

"I can't wear a bullet," she had written to him. "It goes against everything I believe in."

The letter not yet mailed and fat with the unaccepted bullet lay on her dresser in Chapel Hill.

A week after "burying" her brother my mother returned to the university. She opened the door to her damp basement apartment that she has described as walking into a sponge. She told me that the stale must enclosed her and threatened to suffocate her. She left the door open and dropped her bags and immediately went to the dresser and the unsent letter and she opened it and took out the bullet necklace and tied it around her neck. Every evening she took it off and lay it close to whatever bed she was sleeping in and every morning she put it back on. I remember these motions as clearly as I remember her brushing her hair.

My mother says that right after she put on the necklace she began to clean her apartment. She picked up a dishcloth from the kitchen and she spent the entire day wiping the fuzzy gray mold off of record albums and cabinet doors and she spent the evening washing her clothes in the laundromat. She has told me that she was so exhausted that night that she finally managed to sleep, and then she says, "Jimmie wrote me a letter before he died. It came three weeks after the funeral. I never read it."

It doesn't matter that I know all this already. She tells it the same every time, like she is always sifting through the ingredients of her life, trying to figure out what she put in and why. It doesn't matter that she now knows that I used to sneak into her room and pull the letter out of its hiding place, nestled deep into the tee-shirts and long underwear folded in her dresser drawer. I would hold it, turning it over and over, feeling the weight of it and the texture of my mother's name in hard, ball-point script. Sometimes I would lie in bed with it resting on the pillow and my hand resting on it. Uncle Jimmie and his unopened letter were as close as we ever got to religion.

After the story of the bullet and the letter my mother will say, "Two months later I met your father. He wanted a baby and I agreed to have one for him. He was mommy shopping."

She laughs. Her laughter here is as much a part of the story as my father's lank blond ponytail and his lime-green bandanna and the name that he went by. I have told you that Sol is what he called himself. Sol is what everyone, including me, called him. His real name was Albert Masey. My mother met him at a party.

Her friends, Rick and Daisy, came by her apartment late one afternoon. Rick sat on the couch and sifted pot down the spine of a record album. He rolled six joints and lined them up into a fanfare pattern on the coffee table. Daisy took Momma into her bedroom and picked out a long Indian print dress for her to wear. "We're going to a party," Daisy told her, throwing the dress in Momma's direction. It was Momma's dress with the blue elephants marching across its hem.

"I don't want to go to a party," my mother said. She had stopped going to school. She had stopped going anywhere.

"We're going," Daisy told her, and Momma obediently dressed and climbed into the back seat of Rick's old blue Ford station wagon and allowed herself to be driven for miles out into the country.

Momma says that the roads twisted around dairy farms and empty fields. She says that they passed a joint back and forth until it was so short it burned her fingers and that Rick put the roach in his mouth and swallowed it. She says that she settled into the back seat and watched the scenery go by. She looked into people's houses, catching glimpses of other lives — someone opening a cabinet, a woman washing dishes while, from another window, the blue glow of a television shone eerie and cold into the evening. She tells me that she remembers doing this with my Uncle Jimmie. She remembers listening to Jimmie make up stories about the people they saw when they took trips with their parents. She tells me that they would sit in the back seat while their father drove the family to the beach and Jimmie would point to a man raking his leaves and he would say, "You see that man? He is the great-grandchild of another man who was a sailor and killed a dragon." She used to wonder, how does he know these things?

My mother was always thinking about Jimmie in the days after his death and it was no different on the way to the party set high on the hill, the party where she met my father. She has always referred to it as the party set high on the hill and from her descriptions I see them coming around a curve on a dark country road and seeing rows of cars parked on both shoulders and hearing the music filtering through the air. High on the hill my mother saw an old farmhouse with every single light on, a band on the porch, a yard full of people and a large oak tree silhouetted against the brightness from the house.

As they climbed the steep driveway, the band ended its song. There was applause and whooping from the crowd. The guitarist let out a loud, distorted wail of a chord. The lead singer made a sound like a siren. People laughed.

My mother stood at the edge of it all. When she turned around, Rick and Daisy were not there. Someone passed her a joint and she took a draw and then passed it on. Another one came from somewhere else, this one rolled in sweet, pink, strawberry-flavored paper. It was the first time she'd ever tasted strawberry paper and she tells me that she liked it. I used to eat pieces of it, myself.

Momma always says that she smoked some of every joint that landed in her hands and she took a sip from every bottle that passed her way. The way the story goes is that a small blond woman came by carrying a pickle jar. In the bottom of the jar was a layer of dark brown beans mixed in with coins and a few dollar bills wafting around towards the top.

"Donations," the woman said and she shoved the jar towards my mother. Momma started digging around in her purse.

"For me and her," a man said from behind her and his

hand came down and dropped a five-dollar bill in the woman's jar. The blond woman's face brightened and she smiled and drifted off into the crowd. "Donations. Donations."

My mother turned around to see a tall man standing there. She tells me that his blond hair was pulled back into a thin ponytail and his forehead was wrapped in a lime-green bandanna.

"I've never seen a bandanna that color," my mother told him.

"You can have it," he said, taking it off his head and handing it to her. "Do you want to get high?"

"I'm already high."

"You just think you're high," my father replied. The lime-green bandanna was still dangling, unaccepted, in his hand. He reached out and tucked it into the shoulder of my mother's dress and his fingers grazed the bullet that dangled at her throat. He took her arm and steered her towards the oak tree.

What follows is as predictable to me as if it were my own memory. My mother always says, "Your father was like that. He could steer people like they were cars." And then she says,

"He had the best pot I'd ever smoked."

I remember my father but my memories are layered with my mother's story.

My mother tells me that he had "chiseled good looks," and then she goes on to describe the blanket spread beneath the oak tree and the blue-jean jacket and the two red, metal-flake motorcycle helmets.

"My name is Sol," my father said to my mother. "And you are Sara."

Momma will shake her head at this point in the story and she will say to me, "I never found out how he knew my name, but I can tell you this — your father was not a subtle person."

My mother kept the lime-green bandanna. For years it stayed wrapped around the gear shift of her van. When I was younger, I would play with it and she would tell me, "Someday that will be yours."

My father had plans. One plan was to find a cheap house out in the country. Another plan was to start a baby. Another one of Sol's plans was for my mother to drop out of school and so she did. She wanted to anyway, she reminds me. She had not gone to class since Jimmie died. It was June now and classes were over and all my mother had was incompletes. She wasn't going back. She hated her apartment and campus and the nagging phone calls she got from her parents. All my mother wanted to do was ride on the back of Sol's bike, she told me, and at that point in her life she would have done anything to feel the wind in her face.

So Momma got a job in a Mexican restaurant. She wore wide, colorful skirts and blue peasant blouses. Sol started picking her up after work on Saturdays. She got off at three. They would ride his motorcycle for miles out into the surrounding counties and my father would reach behind him and slip his hand under Momma's billowing skirt. He would stroke her leg at sixty miles per hour. He would caress her young thighs while crossing the Haw River bridge on 15-501 South.

It was close to the Haw River that they found the house I was born in. The house was three stories high, without plumbing and full of hay. It sat at the end of a long, washed-out driveway that spoke of abandonment.

My parents talked to a neighboring farmer to find out who owned it. Luke Jones owned it they were told. The farmer pointed down the road. "It's the yellow house down that way."

My parents visited Luke Jones. He shrugged and told them it didn't have running water. Sol offered him thirty-five dollars per month.

"Fifty," Luke Jones said.

"Fifty," Sol agreed.

That day my mother tied the lime-green bandanna around her nose and mouth and went to work sweeping the dirt and hay out of the house. Sol sat outside on the grass and he told her later that the clouds of dust, puffing from the open windows and doors, made it look like the house was on fire.

During the week, while my mother waited tables, my father rode to the house alone. His job was to clean the outhouse. He swept and scrubbed the inside and then painted the outside with a dark blue paint. The wood was so dry that it soaked up three coats before Sol settled for the pale smoky blue it seemed determined to be. He strung multi-colored Christmas lights around the roof line and ran an orange extension cord through the trees towards the house. On the walls he stapled the pictures of the Beatles that had come with the White Album.

The next Sunday, they borrowed a truck and began moving in. Momma had not seen the new, improved outhouse and Sol stole away for a moment to string a red ribbon across the door. With the same red ribbon he hung a pair of scissors so they dangled against the pale blue wood. Inside, on the little bench, he placed a bucket of ice with a chilled bottle of champagne in it, two wine glasses, a joint and a box of Ohio Blue Tip matches.

Just as the sun was setting and the sky was becoming dusky, he blindfolded my mother and guided her down the back steps and across the yard.

"Where are you taking me?" she asked.

My father did not answer.

Momma says that he led her around the house three times before he placed her back on the path that they had been on, the path from the back door to the outhouse.

Momma says that when he pulled the blindfold off of her he was like a little boy. "Ta-da." He swept his arms towards the outhouse. My mother clapped her hands and laughed. The Christmas lights were on, blinking into the darkened yard, casting colored reflections onto the grass. Momma could see the gold flame of a kerosene lamp shining through a knothole in the door.

"Cut the ribbon. Cut the ribbon," Sol said.

My mother ceremoniously picked up the scissors and snipped the ribbon. Behind her she could hear my father making drum-roll noises. They sat together in the little house, Sol perched on the closed toilet seat and Momma in his lap. They shared a joint and kissed and toasted their glasses of champagne to their new outhouse and their new life.

"To our baby," Sol said.

"Hear, hear," Momma added and they clinked their glasses together and threw back their heads, draining the last of the wine. Sol threw his glass out into the yard where it shattered against a rock. Momma threw her glass and it rolled against the mossy side of a tree where it stayed. Years later, I would fill it with sand and pretend that I was drinking champagne like Momma. I would hold a stick in my fingers and draw on it as though it were a joint and I was sucking the smoke deep into my lungs. "To our future," I would say, as I held my glass of sand high in the air. "To our baby. Hear, hear."

This is one of my mother's favorite stories about my father. "This was Sol at his best," she says when telling this story. She smiles when telling this story.

Soon after moving in, my mother quit her job at the Mexican restaurant. She spent the fall roaming fields and back roads, picking the wild yellow daisies that were in bloom all across Chatham County. She set them in jars around the house, on the kitchen table, on the mantle, beside the big iron bed they had bought at a junk store. She even set them in the outhouse and on the hearth in front of the woodstove in the kitchen.

When winter came, my parents cut firewood with a cross-cut saw and stacked it inside the back porch. After one month of this Sol bought a chain saw, a bright orange thing that usually sat in a puddle of oil near the steps. Momma started weaving baskets made of honeysuckle vine and on the day he bought the chain saw Sol also bought her three pairs of clippers for her birthday. She started pulling the vine down from barns and trees. It had to be boiled before Momma could weave with it and she always did this in a big aluminum pot on the kitchen stove.

"Your father always thought it was food," she tells me. "He always walked in and lifted the lid on the pot, only to peer in and find all that vine bubbling away in brown water."

It did smell like food. I remember the smell in the warm, steamy kitchen. I remember looking for hamburgers every time Momma boiled vine.

It was Sol's dope business that supported them and kept them in fresh water. Sol's friends did not show up without rolling papers and rinsed out milk jugs full of clean water. They always left with red eyes and empty jugs. They always returned with full ones.

When there wasn't company to get high with, Sol got high alone and drew pictures on the beadboard walls inside the house. He drew saints, wearing robes and halos and holding odd objects. The one in the kitchen held his hands out and in his cupped palms sat a frog wearing bifocals. The saint of the stairwell had six arms and six hands that held brooms and mops and buckets and rings of keys. The bedroom saint held a baby.

When Momma told my father that she was pregnant, he stopped working on the fourth saint. It was in the living room and it held nothing. Its hands weren't there yet, only its head and its halo and part of its torso, roughly sketched in charcoal. When Momma told Sol that she was pregnant, he went out and bought fifteen cans of paint in seven different colors and he began to paint the floors, each board a different color.

He started with blue. Then he moved on to yellow and Momma knew not to step on yellow. When friends came over she would tell them, "It's yellow this week." Or, "It's purple this week." And the friends would know which color to avoid. Only one person forgot.

"That was Tommy," Momma would tell me, pointing to the red sneaker prints that ran across the ribbons of color on the kitchen floor. The sneaker prints faded away out the back door and were shadow tracks across the porch. "He was no good." Momma always says this about Tommy.

The story that naturally follows is the story of my birth, of Margaret the midwife's long braids that she kept coiled around her head and how both Margaret and Momma begged Sol to get a car before I was born.

He finally did. An old beige VW van that got stuck in the muddy spring puddles that were right in the center of the driveway. Both Sol and Tommy said it was the other one's fault. They argued about it for months and they walked down to the puddles every day and argued some more and smoked dope and shoveled a few watery spadefuls of dirt from behind the tires.

The van stayed stuck and Momma grew big with me and one day Sol came bursting out of the outhouse waving a *National Geographic* in the air. Momma says that she was sitting on the back steps stripping the husks off of vine.

"Look at this," Sol said to her.

She glanced at the magazine in his hands. "My hands are wet," she said. She ran her fingers down a piece of boiled vine, peeling the husk off into a slimy pile at her feet.

"Listen," and then Sol read to her about a tribe somewhere that made a ceremony of burying a newborn's placenta. "Should we do that?" he asked.

"I'd rather have that van unstuck," my mother said.

That was when Sol started digging a hole out in the yard. He chose a spot in the center of three cedar trees and that's how I got my name. "You would think he was burying fifty placentas," my mother has said. "The way he worked on that hole. And when I went into labor, do you know what he said?"

I know exactly what he said. I know the story inside out. I know that Momma was scrubbing the kitchen floors when she first went into labor; I know that her water broke and ran down the purple floorboard towards the woodstove; I know that my father got angry with her for using three jugs of water to scrub the floors with and that Margaret told him to fuck off — Momma could do that if she wanted to — and I know that when my mother told Sol that it was time, he said, "It can't be. I haven't finished digging my hole."

"Thank God it was summer," my mother always says. "And the puddles were dry and the van was delivered. Even though we didn't need it."

My birth went off without a hitch. Margaret and her assistants left instructions for rest and quiet, but as soon as they were gone Sol invited thirty people over to celebrate. At least sixty came. They all signed their names in a guest book, a spiral bound notebook that Sol had purchased just for this occasion. Momma used to look at the book while nursing me at the kitchen table. She used to read off a name and say, "Who's that?" And Sol would be unable to answer.

The night that I was born, my father stripped the bed of its bloody sheets. He wadded them around the afterbirth and he buried it deep in the hole he had dug. And the people who came to my birthing celebration surrounded the grave with rocks.

Momma woke up in the dark morning. "White Room" by Cream was blasting on the stereo. A light from outside flickered against the wall. She got up to pee. Her legs shook as she straddled the bucket and her pee rattled long and hard into its tin bottom. Momma picked me up and carried me to the window. There were people surrounding a huge fire and Sol was lighting a joint. He stuck the lit end into his mouth and circled inside the crowd, waving his arms in a wild dance and shotgunning them, blowing the smoke into their eager faces. I whimpered and Momma opened up her shirt to nurse me.

I was four years old when Momma finally left him.

I remember him holding me up as I painted my pictures on the walls next to his saints. I remember the set of finger-paints Momma bought for me and that Sol and I dipped our hands in and pressed them against the wall above the mantle. I remember Sol calling my mother downstairs and asking her to make a handprint too. He labeled them. Sara, Cedar, Sol.

I remember watching my father pee off the back porch, his urine a yellow arc fueled by beer. I remember, during the summer, Sol and Tommy sitting out in the backyard on lawn chairs, passing a pipe or a joint back and forth. In the winter, they pulled their chairs around the wood-stove. I remember that by the age of four I could roll a good tight joint. Sol paid me a quarter for every one that he approved of.

I remember the game we played called "outside agita-tor." Sol would tie white armbands on both of us and we would march through the house and the yard singing to the Country Joe and The Fish album.

> *And it's one-two-three what are we fighting for?*
> *Don't ask me, I don't give a damn.*
> *Next stop is Vietnam.*

Momma had a new job at a doughnut shop and sometimes she came home to find us playing this game, marching around the multi-colored floors singing and wearing our white armbands. On these occasions, she would laugh and join in. Momma's white armband looked like trim on her pink polyester uniform. She would tell Sol that he was ridiculous and they would hug and kiss while I danced at their feet.

But more often, she came home from the doughnut shop to find Sol passed out on the couch in the living room, the fire completely burnt out in the woodstove and me cuddled deep into my sleeping bag, trying to stay warm. She would come into my room smelling like doughnuts. The skin on her hands and arms would be sticky with sugar. When she finally took off her coat, there would be lint stuck to her arms.

When Momma came home from the doughnut shop, there was a light dusting of flour all over her that made the fine, soft hairs on her face visible.

"Are you alright?" she would ask me.

"Did you bring me a doughnut?" I wanted to know.

Usually she had, a plain glazed doughnut in a shiny white bag. I would sit in bed and eat it while I listened to her clank the door of the woodstove open and crumple paper. Then there was the snapping of twigs, the thud of logs on the floor and soon the crackle of a fire.

Sometimes Momma would wake Sol up and yell at him. Why had he let the fire go out? Why didn't he take better care of me? Why did she have to work while he smoked up his own profits? Why the hell didn't Tommy stay at his house for once?

Other times she would be so angry that she wouldn't wake him up at all. She would count change out of the pocket of her pink uniform and we would go get hamburgers, leaving Sol in a house that was just beginning to get warm and that was usually filled with people and thick with the smoke of cigarettes and dope when we returned.

Momma would tuck me in, but before falling asleep, I would listen to the laughter and conversation coming from the kitchen just beyond my bedroom wall. Sometimes I woke up to the sound of car doors slamming and engines starting and headlights circling my room. I would try to stay awake just long enough to hear Sol go to bed and Momma coming back down the stairs to stoke the stove and check on me.

It was summer when we left.

Two weeks before my fourth birthday, Momma pulled me aside and told me that she and I would be taking a trip together, just the two of us.

"What about Sol?" I asked.

"He's staying here," she said. "And don't tell anyone."

"That he's staying?"

"That we're leaving. Don't tell anyone. Not even Sol."

It took Momma three weeks to get ready. First she took the van to a mechanic and had it tuned up with the money she had been saving from her tips and paychecks. Then she started sorting and washing our clothes, not returning to the drawers and closets the ones she had decided to take with us. Instead she folded the clean clothes and boxed them and hid them in the attic. It meant that my favorite clothes were packed away and I had to wear things I was not accustomed to — dresses and skirts and pants made out of something slick, something that was not denim.

We celebrated my birthday at the ring of rocks where the placenta was buried. I wore a red flowered dress.

I remember Sol laughing and saying to me, "Hey, where's my little tomboy?"

I remember the look that Momma flashed me. It said don't tell. I shrugged and crawled into Sol's lap. I remember his dingy tee-shirt, the smell of his skin, the nicotine stains on his fingers, the soft blond beard that was coming in on his face. He gave me water colors and a new sketch pad for my birthday and then he told me that he got me a new moon.

"A new moon?" I asked.

Sol said yes, a new moon, that we were now the only place in Chatham County with two moons and he took me down to the hardtop road and showed me one bright full moon on the left. When we walked back up the steeply curving driveway he showed me another, identical moon on the right. "Two moons," he said solemnly. "That's what we'll call this place."

Later that night, when Momma was rebraiding my hair in the kitchen and Sol was out on the front porch with Tommy, I whispered, "Momma, are we ever coming back here?"

"I don't know," she said. She yanked the comb through my hair.

"Are we leaving Sol for good?" I asked.

"We don't get along anymore, Cedar. If only he'd do his part without me yelling at him. But even that doesn't do any good."

"Maybe you could teach me his part," I suggested.

"I can't stand another winter here," Momma sighed. "Even his friends don't bring water anymore."

There were twenty milk jugs behind the woodstove. All but three were empty. I knew that tomorrow Momma would toss them in the back of the van before going to work and that she would fill them and bring them home. I knew that tomorrow Tommy would come back. I might earn seventy-five cents rolling joints. I would eat cereal for lunch and Sol would eat a bag of Fritos.

Momma wrapped a rubber band around the finished braid.

"Where are we going?" I asked her.

"West," she said.

"I like the beach," I told her. I remembered that the beach lay east, towards the rising sun. We had driven to the beach the year before. Sol had found a sea gull feather and a crab shell and he had balanced them together into a mobile that hung in my room.

"West," my mother said again. "There's another beach in that direction."

"Can I take the new moon with me?" I asked.

It was a Sunday morning when we left. We snuck away, like thieves. I never got to say goodbye to Sol. He was out somewhere with Tommy.

I was sitting on the back step drawing in my new sketch pad when Momma walked by. She went to the metal trash can that we kept full of birdseed below the dogwood tree. She unhooked the feeder from a branch, filled it and hung it back up. Then she picked up the lid from the garbage can and sailed it into the woods like a giant Frisbee.

"It's time," Momma said, turning back towards me. "Can you help me get the boxes out of the attic?"

I don't think I answered. I think I just looked at her standing in front of the dogwood tree. Her brown hair was braided at the back. Strands had come loose. She was wearing shorts and a tee-shirt. Her legs and arms were strong and tan. The sun was glinting off the brass of the bullet that hung at her throat.

"I'll get them myself," Momma said. She came towards me and she placed her hands on my shoulders. Her fingers gouged into my flesh. She looked me straight in the eye. "Cedar," she said. "I have to do this. Don't give me any shit."

I listened to her climbing the stairs. I heard a bump and a dragging sound and I ran inside and stood at the bottom of the steps, looking up. Soon she appeared at the top of the landing, wrestling with the mattress from the big iron bed. I ran towards the kitchen. I flattened myself against the wall while watching Momma lug the mattress down the stairs and across the living room floor. It flopped to one side and knocked an ashtray off the table. The ashtray clattered and rolled across the floor. Gray dust and cigarette butts spilled onto the rug.

"Goddamn it," my mother said. She held the mattress

steady with one hand and bent down to scoop up the butts. Then suddenly she kicked the ashtray across the floor and straightened up. She hauled the mattress out the door, down the front steps and across the yard to the van. I followed her and watched as she tried to cram the mattress into the side door of the van. She grunted and shoved and pushed. "Get in there, you son of a bitch," she said over and over. "Get in there, you son of a bitch." Finally the mattress popped in and fell over. Momma climbed in behind it and tugged at it until it lay down like a bed that curled up at the edges against the metal walls. She started scraping leaves and grass off of it and throwing them out into the yard. When she saw me standing there, she said, "You need to go to your room and pick out some toys to take with you."

I didn't move.

Momma continued to crawl across the mattress on her knees, tossing out twigs and leaves. She turned and saw me still there. "Hurry," she said.

I ran to my room. I remember the way the sunshine fell across my bed with the rumpled sheets and covers, the crab-shell and feather mobile spinning up above, the white beadboard walls with the peeling paint, my drawings taped above my desk, the tin can of crayons and pencils and brushes that sat next to my notebooks and sketch pads, my teddy bear lying on the blue and yellow braided rug, nestled in among dirty clothes and shoes.

Momma rushed by the door. "Choose," she commanded.

I started rolling up the braided rug with all its mess in it. I tried to drag my desk to the doorway.

Momma whizzed by again, this time carrying a box. "No furniture," she barked. "And get your sleeping bag."

I picked up my teddy bear and my tin can of crayons and pencils and brushes. I grabbed my sketch pads and note-books. I stood up on the bed and yanked the mobile down. And I ripped one of my drawings off the wall. It was a drawing of Sol taking a piss off the porch. I had used yellow crayon and drawn in a splatter where his pee hit the ground. I had drawn in a Budweiser can sitting on the railing. Sol was looking up in this picture, looking up at the sky and smiling as though he was in ecstasy.

"Is this it?" Momma asked when I ran back to the van.

I nodded.

"Good," she said. "You better go pee. We're leaving."

From the outhouse, I looked across the yard towards the kitchen. The pages of my sketch pad were fluttering in the breeze where it still sat on the porch. I could hear the noise they made, an empty noise of pages without people. It was my brand new sketch pad and I left it there.

Momma and I lived in the van, zigzagging our way west for nearly a year. We camped out in national and state parks and on the side of the road. We stopped at every free museum we could find and we saw the world's largest ball of string. We did not hurry and if I said, "Momma, there was a stream back there," she would often turn around and stop and we would go wading. If it was a river I would collect smooth rounded rocks. I would pile them on the shore and before we left I would have to choose. I couldn't take them all. We were traveling light, my mother reminded me.

If we stopped at a lake we would skip stones, counting the jumps they made. Momma showed me how.

"Five," she would predict as she skimmed a stone across the water.

"Four," I would say.

This is how I learned to count, up to seven anyway. That was the record, set by Momma.

Sometimes we would play lion and creep across a field, pretending to hunt. We would climb a tree and the game would change to spy. We would make circles with our fingers, pretend binoculars that we held up to our eyes.

But that was later on, in the middle of the country, after we had gotten used to traveling. At first it was hard. There were nights that I lay wide awake while Momma slept, nights that I shined my flashlight into the back corner of the van, letting its beam bounce off the trickle of water that leaked in during heavy rains. There were nights that I peered out the windows and watched the frogs that were sitting in the middle of the road get smashed under the tires of passing diesel trucks.

Then there were other nights that the moon would be shining so bright neither of us could sleep. We would be parked on the side of a two-lane blacktop and we would have gotten up to kneel on the mattress and peer out the window and watch the house across the street. If it was early morning we might see lights in the house go on and soon, lights in the barn. "Jimmie had a wild imagination," Momma would say. "Jimmie could tell me whole stories about that farmer and his wife. I used to think he knew everything." Her voice would crack and then she would start crying.

I would wrap my arms around her and whisper, "Tell me."

And that's how the Jimmie stories began. I was to hear these stories all my life.

"He went to sailing camp once," Momma told me. "And I was left behind. I never missed anyone so badly. I always felt so lost without Jimmie."

"How old were you?" I asked.

"I was five. He was seven. When he came home he brought me a tiny, little sailboat and we went to the stream behind my parents house and sailed it. But it had been raining and the boat got carried away and we lost it. I cried and cried."

I could feel her shoulders shake and I touched her cheek. She grabbed my hand and held it there.

"Sweet Cedar," she said and then smiled. "Jimmie made me a new boat and I loved it more than the old one."

"Was it pretty?"

She laughed. "No. It was ugly. Just a block of two by four with a pencil for a mast and a paper towel for a sail. But Jimmie had made it. That was all that mattered."

Some nights we sat by a campfire and Momma would pick through and read silently from the box of letters she had carried with us. These were Jimmie's letters, written to her while she was in school and he was in war. The one that was never opened stayed tucked into the edge of this box. She could always lay her hands on it.

"Read it," I would urge. I would be lying next to her with my head on her lap. She would be absently stroking my hair. She would shake her head no and pull another one out and read to herself.

"Is the war still going on?" I asked.

"Yes," she said.

"What are we fighting for?"

"I don't know," Momma would say and she would douse the fire and we would go to bed and in the dim shine of the flashlight my mother would tell me about Uncle Jimmie's funeral and the flag and the empty casket buried somewhere outside of Atlanta, Georgia. She would hold the bullet necklace up in the air, dangling it from its leather thong, and say, "He gave me this."

Some nights it was me that cried. During thunderstorms

all I could think about was our safety. It was too loud inside the van. We had to shout to hear each other. I wanted my house back. I wanted my room. I wanted Sol.

We were two weeks on the road before Momma called him. I stood beside her in a little phone booth that shook with the passing of cars and was filled with traffic fumes.

"Cedar wants to talk to you," Momma said into the phone before handing it to me.

"Where are you?" Sol asked me.

"Arkansas," I answered.

"Let me speak to your mother," Sol said.

It was the last I ever talked to him. Momma yelled into the phone while I stood beside her. I could hear Sol's voice coming through the receiver. I could make out a few words. Home. Cedar. Bitch. My name again. Whore. Momma slammed the receiver down and grabbed my arm. She shoved me into the van and we pealed out of the parking lot. We were on the road again for miles of silence. Momma steered with her left hand and with her right she rumbled around in her big woven bag. When she latched onto her sunglasses she pulled them out and propped them on her nose.

We stopped for gas outside of Little Rock and without saying a word I slid a pair of sunglasses onto the counter and without saying a word Momma bought them for me.

Occasionally we stayed in a town for several weeks while Momma worked and saved money. I liked leaving the towns. I liked getting back in the van and putting on my sunglasses. I liked watching Momma switch gears, check the mirror, change lanes and punch the buttons on the radio, all the while sipping a Coke from the green glass bottle she held between her legs.

Sometimes my mother met a man that she liked and he would travel with us. They would share his tent, pitched beside the van where I would sleep alone, with all the doors locked. I was glad when he turned his truck onto an exit or we let him off on the side of the road to hitchhike in some other direction.

Momma and whatever man would stand on the side of the road at the intersection. I would sit in the van and watch them linger in a long, slow embrace and a passionate kiss. They looked like a postcard with an ever-changing background. Fields of sunflowers in Kansas. Streams in

Wyoming that were bluer than the sky. Hills of aspen and fir in Colorado.

When we pulled away I would wave my hand out the window and let the wind hit against my palm. Momma and I would go out to breakfast. We would talk about where to go next while I sipped a cup of coffee thick with sugar, cream and ice cubes.

It was in May that we were heading into Taos, New Mexico. Just outside of the city, the van sputtered and coughed and a cloud of thick, black smoke poured out of the hood. Momma pulled over and cut the engine off. When she tried to start it again, the key only clicked in the ignition.

We hitchhiked into Taos. I walked backwards like Momma, holding my thumb out to passing cars. When the blue Falcon pulled over for us Momma picked me up and ran towards it. I remember seeing the gravel passing below me. I remember the bump of Momma's purse against my knee. I remember the smile and gleaming brown eyes of the man named Daniel who picked us up. He had curly black hair and a neatly trimmed beard. I remember Momma smiling back and introducing us. I remember Daniel saying to me, "Cedar.

What a pretty name." We lived in Taos with him for three months.

He had an adobe house with a corner fireplace. We had a van that would not run. He had a studio full of canvases and easels and paints and turpentine and a smell that I fell in love with. We had no place to stay. He had a girlfriend named Leah who would not be home for three more months. We did not know that at first, but we had flexibility. And Daniel had an interest in Momma. That was not unusual. Most men did. They were attracted to her tall strong body, her long brown hair and her bright green eyes. I got her height and her muscles and her hair, but I did not get those eyes.

We had been there two weeks before Daniel told her about Leah and by then she was sharing his bed and I was sleeping in the study on the sofa bed. The photographs hanging on the study wall were Leah's. Momma would stare at them after tucking me in and before turning the light off at night. She would stand with her nose to the wall, staring deeply into the black-and-white picture of the woman hanging laundry on a clothesline, just her legs showing beneath the flapping sheets, her body silhouetted in the sun. Momma would move to the next picture, sad-eyed, dark-skinned children standing on the porch of an old shack. The next one, a picture of long-haired men with flowers and peace symbols painted on their faces. The next one, Daniel standing at his easel, a paintbrush in his mouth. The next one, the one that Momma lingered over the longest, a picture of Daniel with his arm wrapped around the waist of a thin dark-haired woman wearing a long paisley dress. They stood on the shore of a lake. Daniel's head leaned towards the woman's. Her head leaned towards his.

Each night Momma looked at the photographs. Each night she looked at this one last and longest. And each night she would turn around to me and say, "Goodnight, Cedar," and flick the light switch on the wall.

My mother got a job within walking distance. She worked the breakfast shift. She wore a shiny orange dress that matched the menus and the tables and the hard plastic benches of the Pancake Castle.

When I woke up in the mornings, Momma would already be gone. Daniel would fix breakfast, and after eating together we would go to the studio. Daniel gave me pieces of cardboard to paint on and he let me use his brushes and paints. We put rock-and-roll on the stereo and cranked it up and he painted at one easel, smoking cigarettes and joints, while I painted next to him at a smaller easel that he had adjusted to my height. I usually did three paintings a day. Daniel worked on the same one all summer. He gave me a smock to wear, one of his old work shirts which I wore backwards. When I got bored, I hung it on a nail in the door, next to one of Daniel's color-smeared aprons. He had six. When I got bored I would go to the living room and watch TV. I had never seen TV before and I could watch it for hours, although Momma didn't like me to.

She got home during the soaps. She would turn the TV off and sit next to me on the couch.

"What's going on?" she would ask me.

"I was watching that," I would complain.

"Did you paint today?" Momma interrupted.

All she had to do was ask about painting and I would forget everything else. I would take her into the studio and show her my paintings. She would kiss Daniel hello. They would hug and oohh and aahhh over my day's work.

It was Leah's house that we lived in rent free. It was Leah that Daniel talked to in hushed tones, late at night. It was always Daniel who answered the phone.

Years later, Momma told me that after we had been there for two weeks and she had slept with him twice, he lay his head on her stomach one night while she played with his dark curly hair and he said, "There's something I have to tell you." He told her that there was a woman named Leah and that it was her house we lived in and that we were welcome to stay for the three months that Leah was away, but if we chose to leave, he would understand.

It was no surprise to Momma. She had seen the pictures in the study. Momma says that she did not stop playing with his hair, that she said nothing at first but thought of me sleeping down the hall and of her job at the Pancake Castle and coming home in the afternoons to find me happy and cared for.

"What does staying mean?" she asked him.

She felt him sigh. She felt his warm breath blow across her bare belly. "I like you," he said. "I like Cedar. But Leah can't find out. We have to end it before she comes home."

Momma says that what she thought of was the broken-down van in the garage six miles away. She thought about money. She thought about living rent free. She thought about Daniel's shirt turned backwards on me and splattered in paint. She ticked these items through her mind, like a list of things to do and then told him she would stay and they made love again.

It may have been because their days were numbered that Momma and Daniel were so sweet with each other. Every night I heard them laughing and talking and coupling and they were pleasant sounds to fall asleep by.

Momma tells me that this is how it happened. This is how we ended up staying together and returning to the house that I was born in. Three days before Leah was due back, two days before we were scheduled to leave, the van was fixed and paid for. Momma and Daniel were playing Scrabble. Momma says that she was winning. She left the room to pee and get more beer and when she returned, the words "I love you" were spelled out across the board. Momma tells me that Sol never told her that he loved her, that he had told her she was beautiful, that he wanted her to be the mother of his child, that they would live in the woods together forever, but he had never said I love you.

"Not that it would have made any difference," she is quick to remind me.

But there it was, all spelled out in Taos, New Mexico. "I love you," in little wooden tiles. And it was that night that Daniel and Momma began planning a life together.

"I want to leave here," Daniel told her. "New Mexico. I want to leave New Mexico."

Momma told him about the house that she had left in North Carolina, the house with the cheap rent and the multi-colored floors and that it might be empty and then again it might not.

"Do you want to go back?" Daniel asked her.

"Cedar loved it and so did I. But what if he's still there?"

"Do you really think he would have lasted a winter without you?"

Momma says that this was the funniest thing she had ever heard, this most obvious question. So obvious that she doesn't know why she never asked it herself.

"We could live with Woody and Elaine," Momma said.

"They'd be perfect. They heat with wood. If they're still around," she added.

In truth, my mother barely knew these people. She had met them in college, through a man she had briefly dated. They had dinner at Woody and Elaine's house one night and Momma had seen that Elaine was a weaver and Woody a potter and she had met the children, who called their parents by their first names, and she had propped her feet up on the hearth of a warm woodstove while drinking hot mulled wine and Elaine had written her phone number on a slip of paper and said, "Call me some time." And Momma did. Once, a year after I was born, another time a year later and again from New Mexico. The cabin that Woody and Elaine lived in was leaking like a sieve and it was too small anymore and they were looking for a new place to live.

It became a plan. Momma would call them when we reached North Carolina and the house with the multi-colored floors. Meanwhile they would start packing. We would start a commune. I would share the attic with two kids named Norther and Roxy. We would share the work. Life would be easy. Life would be very easy, my mother assured me.

And so we left New Mexico. I don't know if Daniel ever said goodbye to Leah but he probably gave no thought to the life that he was leaving and Leah, the dark-haired woman in the black-and-white photograph, probably came home, in living color, to Daniel's empty studio and a love mysteriously lost. Leah would wander through the house, running her hands across the adobe walls and calling his name. She would eventually take down the pictures of Daniel that hung in the study where I had slept and if they had been up long enough, the paint on the wall would be faded all around the blank spaces where the pictures had hung and, no matter how she arranged it, those empty spaces would always be there.

It was August, one day after my fifth birthday, early afternoon and raining like hell the day that we crossed the Haw
River bridge on 15-501 South and began our bumpy jour-
ney up the old driveway, with Momma leading and Daniel
following. The windshield wipers were slapping noisily back
and forth, back and forth, back and forth. I was balancing on
the mattress, watching Daniel fishtail behind us.

"He's gonna get stuck," I said.

Momma whipped the van around a gully and I fell over
sideways. After I had climbed back up, Momma asked, "Is he
still there?"

"I don't see him."

"I can't stop," Momma said as she plowed through more
puddles.

"Here he comes," I said.

I could see the hood of Daniel's blue Falcon as he took
the last of the big curves in our driveway. Momma never let

up on the gas, and when we hit the yard we went right across it, the wet grass slashing against the sides of our van.

The rain was pouring down. The leaves in the woods were glistening a shiny bright green and I remember that everything, including the house, was almost glowing.

We jumped out of the van and ran to the porch and stood there waiting for Daniel. The rain was thundering onto the tin roof.

"It's loud," I shouted.

Momma smiled. "Isn't it great," she yelled back at me. Momma seemed like she was glowing too. She looked up and took a deep breath of air. "It smells good here," she said.

The blue Falcon crested the hill and broke across the yard. When it came to a stop in front of the house, Daniel jumped out. His eyes were wide open. He sank down on the steps and raked his fingers through his hair. "I thought I'd never make it," he said.

Momma laughed. "That was nothing."

"You're going to get wet sitting there," I told him.

"Who the hell laid out that driveway? I've never seen such curves."

"Curves? What about the gullies?" Momma asked.

"We have two moons," I remembered. Momma had explained the curves in the driveway to me, the way that they could trick a person into believing that there were two separate moons. "This is the only place in Chatham County that does, you know."

Daniel got up from the steps and climbed to the porch where it was dry. Water was dripping off his hair and into his eyes. "Two moons?"

"It's what we call this place," I said. I was swinging from the newel posts of the porch, trying to catch raindrops in my mouth.

"Sol named it," Momma said quietly, like she didn't even want to mention his name. "The curves in the driveway. You see the moon to your left coming in and then again to the right. Sol told Cedar that we were the only place in Chatham County with two moons. That was just before we left."

"Is Sol here?" I asked. No one had told me that he wouldn't be. And no one answered me when I asked. I ran up the steps and into the house. It was dark inside. I flicked the light switch, but of course the electricity was cut off. I stood in the doorway letting my eyes adjust to the dimness.

"Sol?" I whispered. "Sol?"

I took a few steps into the living room. My feet left wet tracks in the gauze of dust that covered the rainbow floors. The handprints we had put on the wall above the mantle had a crusty brown smear across them. The stereo and speakers were gone, leaving only a snake of gold wire coiled across one red floorboard.

"Sol?" I whispered again.

"Sol's not here," Momma said from the doorway. "I thought you knew that."

An album cover lay near the window. It was *Layla* by Derek and the Dominos. When I picked it up, marijuana seeds tumbled out of its spine and onto the floor. I remembered my father playing this album every night and falling asleep on the couch. I remembered waking up to the sound of the needle hitting the ride-out groove. It went choopa, choopa, choopa. I remembered the song "Layla." Sol used to sing this song to me. I remembered him dropping to his knees, his face contorted with the imagined pain of unrequited love.

"You didn't think Sol would be here, did you?" my mother said.

I shrugged and let the album cover drop to the floor and looked around me. The sofa stuffing was trailing out onto the rug. The coffee table had been turned over. Beer cans and empty E-Z Wider packs and cigarette butts littered the floor. In the middle of all this was a pile of human shit.

I wandered into the kitchen. Dishes and pans were scattered everywhere, as though someone had hurled them against the walls. Chairs were overturned and spread wildly across the floor. The garbage can overflowed with Hardees bags, crumpled cigarette packs and more beer cans. The kitchen saint that my father had so carefully drawn had a notch in her nose. Next to her, the telephone receiver dangled against the wall. Behind the woodstove sat twenty empty milk jugs.

I went to my old room. Nothing had changed. The desk was still askew where I had tried to drag it out; the rug was still rolled up with my clothes sticking out from its edges. I pushed the desk back where it belonged. I kicked the rug open and a damp moldy smell rose out of it.

Daniel and Momma had followed me through the house and now stood in the doorway.

"I can hang the mobile back up," I said, looking towards the ceiling where the nail was still hammered into the wood.

"The crab shell broke," Momma said. "Remember? You slept on it."

"Oh yeah."

"Cedar." Momma squatted down and took my hands. "It's not going to be the same. It's going to be better."

"I left my sketch pad here," I said, pushing past Momma and Daniel and heading towards the back porch. The back porch was empty except for the rain that blew in across Tommy's faded sneaker prints. I looked towards the outhouse. The orange extension cord still draped through the trees. The path was a muddy slither through the grass. I sank down against the house. The rain slowed to a steady patter. Behind me I could hear Momma and Daniel arguing over who would clean up the shit in the living room.

"I should do it," Momma insisted. "He was my boyfriend."

"Haven't you had enough of his shit?" Daniel asked and

Momma started giggling. I knew they were hugging and I knew the silence of a kiss. Soon Daniel came out and asked me where the shovel was.

"Out there," I said, pointing to the ring of rocks. "That's where my placenta is buried. That's where the shovel has always been."

"I've heard the placenta story," Daniel said. He marched across the yard and came back with the rusty old shovel. He went inside and soon came out with the shit scooped up onto the blade. I followed him to the outhouse and watched him toss it down the hole. The rain started up again.

"We could run for it," I said, looking across the yard to the house.

"Let's wait it out." Daniel sat down on the closed toilet seat and lit a cigarette. "I have something to ask you," he said. "What's your advice to me? How best do I get along with your mother?" He opened his mouth like a fish and blew thick gray smoke rings out into the rain.

"Make sure you stoke the stove in the winter," I told him.

"Is that all?"

"Momma hates to be cold."

Daniel blew more smoke rings. They broke apart like crumbs when they hit the walls or were destroyed by raindrops.

"Will you teach me how to blow smoke rings?" I asked.

"No, you're too young."

"Do you want to make a sign together?" I asked.

"What sort of a sign?"

"Welcome to Two Moons."

"I have to help your mother clean up first," he said.

I nodded and snuggled into the crook of his arm. We looked out the open door towards the house. Momma came out carrying a pan. She stood on the porch calling our names.

"We're in here," Daniel yelled back.

Momma looked through the rain and waved. She dipped the pan into the barrel of water at the edge of the porch. When we returned, she was standing on a chair in front of the fireplace, scrubbing at the brown spot on the wall. Her rag smeared the paint into a blur and when Momma saw that the handprints and names would come off, she scrubbed even harder. I watched the muscles in her shoulders and arms tense as she scrubbed and scrubbed, bending over and dipping the rag in and out of the bucket, until the water was murky and the handprints and the names were gone, leaving a white smear on the dingy beadboard wall. But Momma still didn't stop. She scrubbed harder and harder. Maybe there was something there that I couldn't see.

My mother has told me that it was not idyllic. She has told about the argument she and Elaine had on the very first day of their arrival. They argued over where the pots and pans should hang in the kitchen. Momma thought they should hang where they had always hung, scattered around the kitchen walls on whatever nails were already there. Elaine insisted that they hang above the stove. Momma has told me that she doesn't know why they argued. It was only a matter of hammering in a few more nails. And Elaine was right, my mother told me. The pots and pans should hang over the stove.

None of that is what I remember about the day that Woody and Elaine arrived with their two kids. What I remember is walking down the hill with Daniel to hang up our newly made sign and burying the mail.

We had made the sign the day before, on an old board pulled from one of the barns. In one corner, Daniel paint-ed an evergreen tree with two overlapping quarter moons in the dark blue sky behind it. At the other end, over his carefully drawn lettering, I painted, "Welcome to Two Moons - Inexperienced Drivers Park and Walk."

The 'park and walk' part was Daniel's idea. In fact, it was almost six weeks before he tackled the driveway again.

Daniel nailed the sign to a tree behind the dented blue mailbox. It was me that found the dusty old stack of letters and bills inside.

"The mail's here," I said.

Daniel took the pile from me and flipped through them. "Albert Masey, Albert Masey, Albert Masey, Sara Russel, Albert Masey," he muttered.

"Who's Albert Masey?" I asked.

"Sol's real name. Your father. Cedar, I don't think your mother wants these things in the house. I think we should bury them."

"With what?"

"Well, let's put them under a rock."

"Okay," I shrugged. At the time, it didn't seem so odd. I was sure that if Sol were there, he would have just thrown them in the trash.

I watched Daniel jam a branch under a big rock for leverage. A year later, Norther and I sat back to back on that rock, waiting for the school bus. One day I told him that my father's mail was buried underneath and we tried to turn it over, but we couldn't.

I remember that rock. I remember the hollow spaces in it that were perfect for sitting on. I remember how cold it felt through my clothes while I waited for the school bus. I remember watching Daniel dig a small hole with the claw end of his hammer and the ants scattering across the ground and up his arms. I remember him flicking them off with his fingers. I remember Daniel placing the letters in the hole and with his foot, he shoved the rock back into place.

"Now we have my placenta and my father's mail buried here," I said.

"How's the sign look?" he asked, standing back up.

"It looks good."

"Let's admire it." Daniel put his hand on my shoulder and steered me away from the rock.

It was just then that Woody and Elaine arrived in their red International pickup truck. The back of the truck was piled high with possessions. Mattresses, chairs, and bed frames were the most visible and jabbed in among these things were two children. The truck zipped past us and then came to a screeching halt. The driver leaned out the window. With one hand he steadied his worn felt hat. With the other, he brushed his blond hair from his face.

"Whoops," he yelled back at us. "Are you Daniel?"

"You must be Woody," Daniel yelled.

Woody parked the truck and got out. I remember him and Daniel leaning forward to shake hands. I remember Daniel wiping his hands on his jeans first, wiping away dirt from an overturned rock, wiping away dirt from someone else's buried mail before he would shake another man's hand.

Elaine was as small and friendly as my mother's descriptions of her. She had dark brown braids and wire-rim glasses that scrunched up her nose whenever she smiled. When I think of Elaine, I remember her reaching up with one finger to push her glasses back into place.

All the way from New Mexico to North Carolina, my mother had been describing these people to me. All the way from Leah's adobe house to the driveway of Two Moons,

Momma had been talking about Woody and Elaine and their two children, Norther and Roxy. She had told me about meeting them before Jimmie died, before she met Sol, before she quit school, before a lot of things, it sounded like. She had told me about Elaine's loom and Woody's pottery wheel. She told me about the two children that I would be sharing the attic with. She said to me, as we crossed over the Haw River, followed by Daniel, "At last we'll be living with sensible people. Woody and Elaine know how to keep a house warm."

What I remember about first meeting Norther was his height. He was as tall as I was, plus a few inches. His younger sister, Roxy, was small and thin boned, like a bird. When I first saw them, after Woody stopped the truck, their long brown hair had been whipped into knots by the ride. They jumped down and came over to me.

Daniel gave me a push forward. "This is Cedar," he said.

"Is there a place to go swimming here?" Norther asked.

"There's a stream," I said. I backed up a step and hovered against Daniel's thigh.

"We can dam it up," Roxy said, nodding in Norther's direction. "Make a pond."

"It needs something," Elaine suddenly exclaimed, referring to our sign. She went to the back of their truck and after rumbling around she pulled out an old rubber boot, a hammer and a nail. Elaine bent down and dipped the boot into one of the puddles.

"Nail this up for me," she told Woody. "I can't reach it."

"I just bought these boots at the Goodwill," Woody grumbled, but he nailed it up anyway, just above the sign. His hat fell off his head and he picked it up and slapped the dust off.

"Go pick some of those flowers," Elaine said to her kids, motioning to the goldenrod growing by the side of the road.

"Come on, Cedar." Norther grabbed my hand. "Let's see who gets the most." I shyly followed. As we picked goldenrod, Roxy kept on chattering about how much more she was gathering than me and Norther kept on handing me the flowers that he had picked.

When we handed the flowers to Elaine, she handed them to Woody and he stuck them in the boot. During the entire time that we lived at Two Moons, Elaine kept an ever-changing display of something in the rubber boot. In the spring and summer, it was flowers. In the fall, it was a bouquet of red and yellow leaves. In the winter, it was shiny green holly with bright red berries.

The other boot was also put to good use. I remember it floating around in the rain barrel. We used it for dipping water to dump on the herbs that Elaine grew in coffee cans on the back porch.

Woody offered us a ride up the hill and Daniel crammed into the front seat of the truck, all the while issuing warnings about not stopping. I climbed into the back with Norther and Roxy. We sat among the blankets and chairs turned upside down and sideways, beds and a tent, pots and pans and dishes rattling around. Woody slammed the truck up the hill, not slowing down for anything. As shy as I was, I still laughed uncontrollably when we hit a bump and I saw Norther fly up into the air like a giant rag doll. A box of dishes slid across the bed of the truck and crashed into one wall and Roxy started laughing. Mud was slinging up the sides and splatting all over us. It was the first of many such truck rides, and when we reached the house Elaine took one look at us and told us to go clean off in the stream.

By the end of the day, the three of us were best friends

and Two Moons had been transformed. The truck was unpacked and my bed had been moved into the attic along with Norther and Roxy's. Momma's collection of honeysuckle baskets had been relocated to one of the barns. Elaine's big six-harness loom was installed in the living room in front of the fireplace. Woody's pottery wheel was moved into another barn and he spent an hour laying out sticks to show the exact location of the kiln he would build. The kitchen was in perfect order and the pots and pans were hung on the wall above the stove and there was a pot of rice and beans bubbling on one of the burners.

That was the night that I became a vegetarian. Elaine would not allow meat in the house and she cooked most of the meals. Every day there was something interesting on the stove or in the oven or sometimes both. The kitchen came alive under Elaine's magic touch and to tell you the truth, even though Momma wanted to live with sensible people, I think she was also a little jealous. It seems like the air was always filled with the scent of Elaine's cookies and vegetable stews and beans and bread. Years later, I jokingly referred to our commune as Two Moms.

I used to try to watch bread rise. I would sit at the kitchen table watching Elaine knead the dough and then place it in her big yellow bowl with the blue stripes at the top. She would cover it with a cloth and I would sit there, waiting and watching. But of course I would get bored and go outside, and by the time I came back in, the kitchen was clean and three fat loaves sat cooling on the window sill and I could hear the creak of Elaine's loom coming from the living room.

The weather started getting cooler and Daniel and Woody chopped and stacked wood all day long. The woodpile grew and grew. Every day I thought surely that's enough for the winter and every day they sawed and split and stacked more wood. For weeks, I could hear the buzz of Woody's chain saw off in the woods, then the crack of Daniel's axe. The woodpile started off as a stack between two trees and it grew from there to another stack between another two trees and from there to another two trees. Woody and Daniel covered the piles with old tin roofing and plastic table cloths and shower curtains found at the thrift stores. Woody and Daniel covered the woodpiles with anything they thought would keep it dry.

Norther, Roxy, and I got the very important job of gathering kindling. Dry kindling. We spent two days scouring the woods for dead branches which we hauled into the yard and snapped down to stove size. We stacked them as neatly as the woodpiles were stacked. We stacked them against the back wall of the kitchen porch.

As the days grew colder, we began our vigil of checking the kindling pile and replacing any that had been used. Norther became obsessed with the weather, and if rain was being called for we gathered twice as much kindling.

By late September, the woodpile had grown until it zigzagged across the yard from tree to tree, like a connect-the-dots game that was in my coloring book. Daniel and Woody had stapled plastic over the windows and it depressed me to have the outside views taken away from us.

"It will be warmer," Momma said, in answer to my whining. She laid her hand on my head. "We need all the help we can get."

Momma hated to be cold and the weather was steadily freezing now and we had closed off the kitchen from the rest of the house. As for me, I was getting used to regular meals around the sawhorse and plank table. I was getting used to sharing the attic with Norther and Roxy. I was getting used to Elaine's perfectly seasoned food.

One night we were just finishing our evening meal. The table was spread with plates and dishes and wadded up napkins. Woody went outside to get more firewood. When he came back in, a cold breeze followed him through the back door. I felt it blow across by back. I heard Woody kicking the door shut. I heard the wood being dumped on the floor. I heard the familiar creak of the stove door.

"It's cold tonight," he said.

"Record low today," Norther replied.

"Oh yeah?"

"That's what Tom French on Channel Five said."

Elaine scraped her chair across the floor and began to get up.

Momma reached out and placed the palm of her hand on the table. "Sit back down," she said. "I have something to say. Woody? Will you join us?"

Woody clanked the stove door shut and sat at the table. Momma reached to one side of her and took Daniel's hand

and to the other side, she took mine. "I'm pregnant," she said.

Suddenly everyone was on their feet hugging Momma, but it was Daniel who got to her first. He wrapped his arms around her and squeezed and then he pulled me into this embrace.

I remember that night. I remember the sounds of Elaine and Momma washing the dishes in the corner. I remember the low, intimate murmurs of their conversation. I remember falling asleep in Daniel's lap while Woody read out loud *The House At Pooh Corner*. I remember Daniel carrying me upstairs to bed and tucking me in goodnight and I will never forget the puffs of white that my breath made into that cold attic air.

CHAPTER SEVEN

Margaret the midwife's number was still conveniently scrawled on the wall between the phone and the kitchen saint and Momma called her the next day. She visited us the following week with two other women who would be assisting her. Margaret's hair was still in long braids and still wound tight around her head, just the way that Momma had always described her.

She hugged my mother and then came over to the table and sat beside me. "Hello, Cedar," she said. "I'm Margaret. I delivered you." She pulled on one of my braids and smiled. "You sure got tall," she said. Margaret had a comforting smile. She spread her hands across the table as if to say nothing there, like a magician, and then she began her interview with Momma and Daniel. She seemed most concerned about the running condition of our cars, the driveway, and if we planned to have a party immediately following the birth. Momma and Daniel assured her, again and again, that we did not.

Elaine told me that pregnant women glow. I would make Momma go into a dark room with me and I would close the door, but she never glowed. Momma seemed the same to me, but something seemed to change in Daniel. He became enamored of Momma's stomach. He nicknamed Momma, Kanga, and the baby, Roo. I remember him cupping his hands around his mouth and leaning close to Momma's belly and saying, "Helloo, Roooo. When are you coming out of there?" Momma would laugh and place her hand on Daniel's curly black hair as he leaned his head against her. I remember Daniel plowing up the driveway in Woody's truck, returning from a Saturday yard sale, hauling home an old orange-painted rocker and a crib.

He spent months on the newspaper-covered back porch, wearing yellow rubber gloves and slathering thick blue paint thinner onto the orange wood of the rocker and crib. I watched him scrape away the top layer of paint only to find red beneath it. After that it was yellow, then green, then blue, then red again, until finally he reached the wood and the newspaper was worn and wet and covered with globs and flecks of different colors. I accidentally stepped in it and added my footprints across the kitchen floor, going in the opposite direction of Tommy's red ones.

Daniel sanded and toothbrushed the loose paint from between the spools of each piece. Then he lovingly oiled them and presented them to Momma.

I watched Daniel and Woody carry the crib up the stairs and place it at the foot of the big iron bed. Momma was already sitting in the rocking chair. She was rubbing her hands over the fine, polished wood and pushing the rocker into motion. An electric heater glowed and hummed at her feet. Her hair fell across her breasts and rested on the mound of her stomach. Daniel leaned over and kissed her.

I stood in the doorway. They were like a picture that I wanted to paint and live inside of.

When we talk about Two Moons, Momma will always, always remind me that it was not perfect. She will say it just like that. "Well, it wasn't perfect, you know." She urges me to remember how cold the rooms were outside of the kitchen. She urges me to remember the scary walks to the outhouse at night. She urges me to remember the mice turds scattered behind the dishes.

And I do remember these things. What I also remember is the winter passing with Margaret's visits and watching Momma's stomach grow. I remember Christmas with a lopsided tree hung with cookies and thrift shop ornaments. I remember watching Daniel saw that tree down and seeing the holes in his old leather work gloves and knowing that he had a new pair wrapped and hidden beneath my bed. I remember the kitten Momma gave me for Christmas. Roxy named her Bouncey. I remember laughter and good food and the clank of spoons and dishes every night at the dinner table. I remember books read out loud around the radiant warmth of our woodstove and the way that I would stretch my feet out towards the hearth.

Momma had started gathering and boiling vine again. She was selling her work to a shop in town that also took Elaine's weavings and Woody's pots. During the winter, she moved her basket weaving to the middle of the kitchen floor although she continued to stash the finished product in the barn. By March her stomach was so large that she could barely bend over and she abandoned the enterprise until after the baby was born.

"Much to Elaine's relief," Momma says.

Elaine did not like the basket weaving in the middle of the kitchen floor. It was wet and messy. Momma did it anyway because, during the winter, there was nowhere else to go.

During the winter, there was nowhere else for any of us to go and we all crowded together in the warm kitchen doing our opposite things. Elaine would be trying to cook while Momma sat in a heap of vine and water in the middle of the floor and I painted at the table. Norther watched the weather report on the small black-and-white TV that sat on a stool in the corner. Woody and Daniel alternately brought in loads of wood and stoked the stove and alternately sifted pot and rolled joints at the table while talking about spring and when it might come and if the woodpile would hold out. All the while, Roxy sat close to the stove with a music book balanced on her knees. She was trying to learn how to play the ukulele she had gotten for Christmas. She would carefully position her fingers into a chord and then strum and then try again and again and again. There were days that I was sure her ukulele and Norther's TV and all the chatter appeared on my painting as a black border of off-key notes.

Maybe this is what my mother means when she says it was not perfect. Woody called it cabin fever. All I know is that, when there came a warm day, we would scatter apart like broken glass.

Maybe this is why my mother will remind me of all the other things. She will sometimes tell me that Elaine was a perfectionist and that she felt uncomfortable in the kitchen. She will sometimes say that Woody was too altruistic, operating from some ancient guilt, according to my mother. He was always bringing strangers over for dinner or to stay a few nights in our extra room.

I remember that — an array of different people, at different times, none of whom we got to know too terribly well, except for Topaz.

Topaz was one of the ones that was, supposedly, just passing through. Woody met her at the food co-op. I don't know how Woody managed to meet people and within minutes know that they needed a place to stay and within seconds more invite them to our house. But he did. It was one of his many talents, Elaine said.

Topaz entered our lives one week before my sister was born. It was April and the air had been balmy and warm for nearly three days. We were sure that spring had arrived and we opened all the doors and walked around the house ripping the filmy plastic off the windows. Woody folded it carefully and stacked it on the back porch. I watched him. I remember the crinkle of plastic and the morning sun catching in the sheets as he folded them.

I remember Daniel moving Momma's tubs of water and vine from the edges of the kitchen to one of the barns, even though she said that she was too fat to weave.

He hung her clippers on nails across the wall and he built her a small, low bench so that, when she could weave again, she wouldn't have to sit on the floor.

Elaine spent the day laying out the garden, marking its boundaries with sticks and lengths of string and drawing a map of beans and tomatoes and onions and peas and carrots. Elaine was so anxious to garden that she insisted Woody break the soil that day. I remember watching Woody inside the stringed area, chopping at the ground with a pick axe, the clods of dirt a rumpled brown section in a smooth green lawn. Bouncey lay at the edge of it with both her front paws resting on the cool, brown earth.

I wandered all morning from activity to activity and I spent the afternoon with Norther and Roxy, trying to make that pond we had been planning.

All winter long we had been drawing sketches of the pond and plans for the huge dam that we would be building. As winter progressed, so did our plans until these sketches also included lists of things that we wanted to live there. The lists read, "Turtles, beavers, fish, tadpoles, frogs, mermaids."

The pond was planned for the widest, slowest-flowing part of the stream. We hauled and stacked rocks across the water and packed them with leaves and mud and pine needles. By the end of the day, we had succeeded in creating a pool that measured a few feet across and was filled with dark, muddy water.

"It's not even as big as the puddles in the driveway," Roxy said. Roxy really wanted a pond.

"It'll get bigger if it rains," Norther told her.

"Is it calling for rain?"

"No. Not this week."

We returned to the house dirty and tired, as did Woody and Elaine and Daniel. The only one of us who seemed to be clean was Momma.

The night air was turning cool and we closed all the doors and windows. Woody built a small fire to bathe by and one by one we sponged off in the galvanized tub. No one had cooked that day, so we drove the van into Chapel Hill for one of our rare pizza trips.

We crowded around a big table spread with a red plastic cloth. I remember the booths and tables around us filled with the laughter and chatter of college students. Two pitchers of beer sat on our table. I remember the foam clinging to the glass sides of the pitcher after the beer was gone and I remember the foam clinging to Daniel's moustache and Momma wiping it away with a napkin. Woody handed us some coins for the jukebox.

"Play something good," he hollered, as Norther and Roxy and I crowded around the brightly lit machine.

I watched the records spin around and one drop into place. I watched the heavy arm position itself and then I heard Janis Joplin's gravelly voice singing about Bobby McGee.

When we got home, Topaz was sitting on our front porch, bathed in the yellow glow of the bug light.

CHAPTER EIGHT

Topaz had one leg tucked up under her and was pushing the porch swing in a crazy, uneven pattern with her other leg. She was olive skinned with straight, jet-black hair that just brushed her shoulders. She wore a V-neck, white tee-shirt stretched tight across her breasts, wheat-colored jeans and knee-high, blue suede boots. Between her fingers she held a slim white cigarette with a thin trail of smoke rising into the night air.

She did not get up when we piled out of the van. She waited on the porch and continued to kick the swing in that dizzying, uneven pattern. She took a draw on her cigarette and let the smoke escape her mouth and creep into her nose. She continued to sit there as Woody introduced us all. Her nails were painted flawlessly red and they raked the air when she said, "Hi," and sort of waved to us.

"Topaz is an awfully pretty name," Roxy said. She was staring at the blue suede boots.

Topaz followed her stare. "I've been brushing the mud off my boots from that stupid driveway," she said. "Anyway, Topaz is the name I gave myself. It means blue. Blue's my favorite color. Do you have a favorite color?"

"Topaz is a gem," I told her. "And it's yellow."

I don't know where she got her information from. Just that morning, I had been painting in my room, and when Daniel came in I playfully streaked his nose with the Topaz Yellow acrylic that was on my brush.

"Well, blue is my favorite color," Topaz said.

"Cobalt is blue," I replied.

"I'm tired," Momma said from behind me. "I'm going to bed." She kissed Daniel goodnight and rubbed me on the head. "I can't lean down to kiss you," she said. "I'm too big."

"We can solve that." Woody lifted me up in the air to kiss Momma and then set me gently back down. Momma waddled into the house. The screen door slapped shut behind her.

"Just one more week," I heard her saying to herself.

"You can sleep in the middle room upstairs," Elaine said, following my mother into the house. "Did you bring anything with you?"

"I left my suitcase at the end of the driveway. Will you help me get it?" she said, looking at Daniel.

"I hope you brought a sleeping bag," Woody said. "We don't have any extra sheets." He too let the screen door slap behind him and was gone into the darkness of the house.

Norther and Roxy and I stood out on the porch and watched Daniel open the passenger door of his Falcon for Topaz. We watched him turn around in the yard and we watched the red taillights disappear into the woods.

"She sure is pretty," Roxy said.

Topaz slept all morning and didn't get up until after lunch time. That afternoon, when I passed the extra room, I saw that she had hung posters on the walls. Even from where I stood at the top of the stairs, I could see that most of them were slightly askew. There was a scarf draped across the window and a small cone of incense was smoldering on top of a beer can. Topaz was standing on a chair screwing a blue light bulb into the socket. "Hi," she said when she saw me standing there. "Do you like it?"

"Your posters are crooked," I told her.

Downstairs, Woody was sitting at the table, quietly drinking a cup of coffee and rolling a joint while Elaine slammed around behind him, rattling and banging pans and dishes.

"Just passing through, my ass," she muttered. "She's decorating the goddamn room."

I picked up an apple and went outside.

Roxy was just coming down the path from the outhouse. "Topaz is going to help me paint my nails," she said.

"I could have helped you paint your nails," I told her. "Between me and Daniel, we must have all the paint in the world."

"It's not nail polish. It's not the same thing."

Momma paid no attention to Topaz. Momma was too pregnant to care about anything, except birth. She waddled around the house, ignoring us all, sinking into chairs and sighing, then heaving herself up to do some small task before she was too tired again.

She did not notice or care that Roxy got all her fingernails and toenails painted a bright red, although it certainly didn't escape Elaine's attention. She did not notice or care that Topaz stole the television up to her own room. She did not notice the tension between Woody and Elaine that surfaced the day that Topaz hung her crooked posters. And when Woody asked Topaz one night at dinner how long she planned to stay and Topaz replied by complaining that it was too noisy to write her poetry in this house, Momma did not seem to notice or care that Daniel offered to help Topaz fix up one of the small outbuildings for a writing hut.

Momma was focused on one thing and one thing only and that was the life that she carried inside of her. Every night she told us that she was ready. As she heaved herself up the stairs to bed, she would say, "Maybe tonight."

Daniel would rub Momma's stomach and say, "Now, Sara. Be patient. The baby's just ripening."

And Momma would snap his head off. She was definitely ready. My sister was born during a sudden snow storm in April, two days before the anniversary of my Uncle Jimmie's death. We didn't know the snow was coming. We had been stealing the TV back from Topaz only to have it disappear again. This was one of the days that Topaz had it, and without the TV in the kitchen we hadn't listened to the weather report. We did know that it had turned cold again and we cursed our arrogance in taking the plastic off the windows and we built our first fire in over a week.

I remember that the sky was still clear and the moon full when I went to bed. I remember that Momma had scrubbed the floors the day before. I remember waking up to the sound of a car skidding up the hill and the sight of its headlights circling the ceiling. It was Margaret arriving with her entourage of helpers, in a truck driven by her boyfriend and weighted down heavily with a bed full of rocks.

I watched my sister come into this world. Momma gave birth in the kitchen on the sofa cushions that were pulled close to the woodstove. Daniel named her Patina but we called her Baby Roo. Margaret took a Polaroid picture and it stayed propped on Momma's dresser. Momma and Daniel and myself were looking proudly into the camera, with Baby Roo latched onto one dark nipple.

It was early morning. The snow had accumulated to six inches and it still quietly drifted down. Everyone was up except for Topaz. Elaine brewed coffee and served it to the crowd of midwives and friends at the long table. Woody filled the bird feeder outside the window and stoked the stove. I remember listening to the birds arguing over the feeder. I remember hearing the crackle of the fire and the murmur of conversation at the table. I remember the scent of coffee lingering with wood smoke and birth smells. I remember Bouncey curled up behind the woodstove, nestled in among the water jugs. I remember the warmth of the kitchen and watching the snow drifting outside the window and I remember falling asleep on the sofa cushions with Daniel and Momma and my new baby sister, Roo.

Almost two weeks later the Vietnam war officially ended. Topaz was not home so we stole the TV back and crowded around it in the kitchen and watched panic-stricken people grabbing and shoving to get onto helicopters, the wind from the blades whipping their fine black hair into their faces. Momma sat in the rocker, nursing Baby Roo, tears streaming out of her eyes, no sobbing. Daniel stood behind her with his hand on her shoulder. Woody stood behind Elaine with his hand on her shoulder. Norther, Roxy, and I crowded together on the floor. No one spoke. The only sound was the news report and the screams of the people in Saigon and Baby Roo suckling at Momma's breast.

They say the "summer of love" was in 1969, but for Momma and Daniel, Woody and Elaine, Roxy, Norther, and me, it was 1975. The birth of Baby Roo and maybe the end of the war brought us together like we had never been before. Roo was not just Momma's and Daniel's baby. She was our baby. We took delight in everything she did. We participated in everything she needed. There wasn't one of us, except for Topaz, who didn't change diapers, warm bottles, or coo and cradle. We would have nursed her if it had been within our capabilities, but of course it wasn't. Only Momma could do that.

After Roo was born, we forgot about Topaz. Daniel forgot his promise to fix up a writing hut. Roxy let the polish on her nails chip and peel away. The tension between Elaine and Woody seemed to get buried in the garden with the seeds they planted and it seemed like they fell in love all over again. I often saw Woody and Elaine out in the garden, leaning on hoes and kissing among the yellow flowers of the tomato plants.

It was a summer filled with ticks and mosquito bites, fresh vegetables from our garden, plenty of rain pounding on the tin roof and lots of smooching. Woody and Elaine were smooching. Momma and Daniel were smooching. And no one knew it, but Norther and I were smooching too. Late at night, after Roxy went to sleep, Norther would crawl into my bed beneath the only attic window. If the moon was full, we would look out into the yard and sometimes see the huge barn owl that lived in the woods, swooping down after a mouse. Norther and I would talk and cuddle and kiss and that would be all. When I fell asleep, he would sneak back to his own bed and the next day there would be new games to play, new pictures to paint, and our pretend garden to tend. Our pretend garden was staked out next to the grown-ups' garden and in it we grew rocks and sticks and weeds, all laid out into carefully straightened rows.

Momma has said that she thought we were happy. What she means is that she thought she and Daniel were happy. I thought so too. I try to remember the things that went wrong that summer.

There was the week that Roo got the croup and her thin, tinny wail wound itself into everything we did, but that was only a week. There was the fact that Norther and I both started first grade at the end of August and that we endured taunts from other children for being "the hippie kids." We hated school, but once we were home, everything seemed okay. There were other things that went wrong, but nothing big. Elaine burned her leg when she dropped coffee in her lap. I skinned my knee running down the driveway. Roxy got glass in her foot when we went into town and Norther got stung by a wasp in one of the barns. I remember that Woody smashed his thumb with a hammer and the nail got dark and finally fell away, leaving a soft new nail underneath, and Daniel drank too much one night and threw up in the bushes outside the back porch.

But these things were nothing. They were the things that had always happened. They were not enough to make a man unhappy. I have listened to Momma turn it over and over in her mind and think out loud, "Maybe it was the croup. Maybe it was Roo's constant crying. Maybe it was winter. Maybe it was . . ." and her voice would trail off into nowhere.

I don't think it was any of these things. I think it was Topaz, plain and simple.

I hardly noticed her all summer long. She slept late and never ate with us. Occasionally I would see her stumbling to the outhouse in the early afternoon or sitting in the kitchen eating leftovers. She went into town nearly every day and sometimes I saw her walking down the driveway towards the road to hitchhike out. Sometimes she didn't return for days and I would think to myself that she had finally left. But then I would see her, trudging up the driveway in her blue suede boots. She always wore her blue suede boots, no matter how hot it got.

In the fall, she stopped going into town every day and she began joining us for meals, although she never joined in on the preparation of them. Momma has told me that Topaz never contributed anything to our household. I don't know why this was attractive to Daniel. I don't know why she was allowed to stay as long as she was. I don't know why we listened politely when she sat at our table during dinner and heaped fried rice onto her plate and again complained about the noise in the house and how it interfered with her work.

What she meant was that she could not write her poetry in our house. I don't know why we listened and I don't know why Daniel once again offered to help her fix up an out-building as a writing hut, but I do know that this time Momma took notice.

"When do you plan to do that?" Momma asked.

"Is Saturday okay?" Daniel asked Topaz. She was passing him the bowl of rice.

Topaz nodded and smiled.

Momma fell silent. She watched Daniel fill his plate. When he handed the bowl to her, she asked if he could serve her because she was holding Baby Roo in her lap. Daniel served her, but every time a new dish came her way, he had to be asked again. Momma held a fork in her right hand and fed herself. She jostled Baby Roo on her knee and occasionally spooned something soft into her mouth.

"Daniel," Momma said. "There's a craft show in town on Saturday. You promised to help me with Roo. You said you might sell some of your paintings."

"It seems a shame to sell such beautiful paintings," Topaz said. "At least with a poem you get to sell it and keep it."

"Sunday then," Daniel said to Topaz.

"Have you sold any poems?" Elaine asked.

"I almost did," Topaz said. "But I slept late that day."

"I'd love to read your work sometime," Daniel told her and he smiled at Topaz. It was the same smile he gave to Momma when he picked us up hitchhiking in New Mexico.

I guess Daniel did read Topaz's work. I remember them sitting outside on the steps of the back porch, flipping through sheaves of notebook paper together. I remember the disheveled stack of papers Topaz held in her lap. They were as crooked as the posters in her room, and when a wind lifted some and sent them scooting out into the yard, I remember Daniel retrieving them for her. And I know that Momma remembers this too.

This scene is wound into the stories she tells, and, besides, I saw her standing at the screen door watching with Roo propped on one hip. Elaine came up behind her and peered over her shoulder. She sighed and shook her head and went back to her cooking. Momma turned away. She sat at the table next to me and lifted her shirt for Roo. "I don't know what the fascination is," she muttered.

That night, Momma wore a long print dress to dinner instead of her usual overalls. Her soft brown hair fell across her back in waves left over from the braids she had recently brushed out.

"You look beautiful," I told her.

"Thank you, Cedar." She smiled. "This is the dress I was wearing when I met your father." She smiled again and slid into a chair.

I fingered the thin, soft material of Momma's dress. I touched the blue elephants marching across the hemline. "No wonder he wanted you to have his baby," I said.

I don't know how Daniel could not have noticed Momma that night, but he sat right next to her and talked about his plans for Topaz's writing hut and he did not feel the pall that fell over us like a thick, suffocating blanket. None of us said anything and Daniel kept on talking and Topaz kept on asking questions about windows and light and how would he do this or that and suddenly Momma's chair scraped across the floor. She rose up with Baby Roo in her arms and she turned away and she left the table. We listened to her feet on the stairs. We listened to the door slamming in its frame. We heard Baby Roo start crying from up above.

That night Woody tucked me in and I could hear the argument from Momma and Daniel's room. "Jealous," he said. "Relax," he said. "You're overreacting," he said.

I could hear Momma's soft voice between his words, but I couldn't tell what she was saying. The only clear words I could hear were Daniel's and they were loud and defensive. "I can't believe you don't trust me," he said.

A muttering from Momma.

An interruption from Daniel. "After all we've been through. This really tells me something about you, Sara."

It rained hard that night. I was startled awake by a loud clap of thunder and I lay listening to the deafening downpour on the tin roof only inches from my head.

"Are you awake?" I said into the darkness but no one answered. The room occasionally glowed with flashes of lightning and then I felt a plunk of water on my arm. Another flash of lightning and I could see the stream of water glistening above me on the boards of the ceiling and then another plunk fell onto the covers of my bed.

The storm helped to light my way down the stairs and into the hallway towards Momma and Daniel's room. A flash of brightness and I saw the closed green door to Woody's and Elaine's room and then it was dark. I inched forward, my hand gliding along the wall and into an open doorway. Another gleam of lightning and for a brief moment I could see into Topaz's room, the bare, empty mattress on the floor, the crookedly taped rock-and-roll posters, the ashtray on the bed and, beside it, an empty wine bottle lying on its side.

I inched along and opened the door to Momma's room and bright rivers of lightning burned the scene forever in my mind. Momma was standing at the window looking out in her long blue nightgown, her thick braid of hair falling down her back and Roo in her arms.

"Momma, it's leaking over my bed," I said.

She turned and looked at me, slow-motion, ghost-like. She nodded. "Did you move your bed?" she asked flatly.

I shook my head no and walked to the window beside her. We both looked outside. There was a boom of thunder and a blaze of lightning and down below, on the grass in the rain, I could see two naked bodies making love, Topaz lying beneath Daniel, his dark, wet hair stuck to his back, his ass humping up and down, her legs raising and wrapping around his back, her hands reaching behind her and clutching one of the rocks that circled the grave of my placenta. I felt my mother's thin fingers gripping my hand and I looked up at her. Her eyes were gazing steadily out the window.

The crashes of thunder and the lightning roaring through the sky were as wild as the fucking that was going on below. Daniel's ass went up and down. Topaz arched her back. Her hands pushed the rock from my placenta grave off into the yard. The wind whipped the trees, back and forth. Pink and gold lightning streaked the sky and, for the first time in my life, I prayed.

Please storm, kill them, strike them down.

After Momma moved my bed away from the leak, I sat listening to the roar of water falling onto the tin roof, listening to the thunder cracking through the night, listening for the sound of footsteps on the stairs and listening for the words my mother would say to Daniel. No matter how I strained to hear them, I couldn't. The storm was too loud.

It was early morning when Momma came in carrying Roo. I was ready for her. I had pulled a dresser drawer out and padded it with my softest clothes and when Momma came in, I took Roo from her and laid her in the drawer, tucking tee-shirts and pajamas close around her. Roo looked at me with big, wide baby eyes. She reached her chubby little hand out and wrapped her fist around one of my braids.

"It's okay," I told her as I pried her fingers loose. "It's okay."

Roo shook her head from side to side, but she didn't cry.

"Are you okay?" I asked Momma.

"He won't even talk to me," she said.

Momma crammed herself into my little bed and tugged the covers over her feet. She pulled a joint and a pack of matches from her bathrobe pocket. I sat in a rocking chair beside the bed and I watched the flame of the match fizz quickly and then the glow of the joint as she smoked. Halfway through, she stubbed it out on the windowsill and then lay down. She stared at the ceiling and I sat in the rocker, staring at her. We didn't talk. The storm slowed down to just a patter and then stopped. The house creaked. The sky turned a rosy pink and the sun came up. Down below I heard Woody and Elaine getting up. I heard their soft footsteps on the stairs and then noises from the kitchen and soon the smell of coffee drifting through the house. Momma just lay there.

"Do you want me to get you some coffee?" I asked.

She didn't answer.

Soon Woody came bounding up the stairs. "Up, up, up, little ones," he sang out, as he did every morning. "Rise and shine."

"Shhh." I held my finger to my lips and pointed to

Momma, whose eyes were wide awake. Then I pointed to Roo, sleeping in the drawer, trying to justify the quiet I wanted.

"What's going on here?" Woody asked. "Where's Daniel?"

"Fucking Topaz," Momma said.

"What?"

"The bastard fucked Topaz last night, out in the yard. I saw him. He says I'm crazy."

"I saw him too," I said.

Woody lay his hand on my shoulder. "Have you been up all night?" he asked.

"Not all night," I said.

"No school," he told me. "You stay home." Then he went to his own children's beds and quietly shook them awake. "Get dressed," he whispered.

Behind me I could hear Norther and Roxy getting dressed, the rough swish of blue jeans being pulled on and the sound of snaps clasping shut. But I kept facing Momma and when Roxy asked what was going on, I didn't answer. I heard Norther shush her and, before they left, he came over and pressed something cold into my hands. When I opened

my palm to see what he had left me, I saw that I was holding his lucky stone, a clear quartz crystal that he had found
in the driveway one morning. I held it to my forehead. It felt
cool and soothing and so I held it to my heart. I thought of
Topaz reaching behind her and clutching the stones of my
placenta grave and I got up and crawled into Norther's bed.
When I heard the quiet deep breathing coming from
Momma that I had been listening for, I finally slept too.

Momma slept all day, but I woke up late morning. I went
to my placenta grave and I replaced the one rock that had
rolled away and then I spent part of the day cradling Roo in
the kitchen and watching Elaine fix dinner. I spent the other
part of the day sitting on Momma's bed watching Daniel
pull his clothes out of the dresser and toss them beside me.

"I saw you," I said.

A tee-shirt landed beside me.

"I saw you," I said again.

A pair of jeans.

"I saw you. I saw you. I saw you," I started chanting and
the faster I chanted, the faster he worked until the clothes
were flying out of his hands and hitting the mattress in crazy

time with the maniacal rhythm of my chanting. Daniel scooped his bundle of tee-shirts and jeans into his arms. I followed him to the door and, still chanting, I watched him walk down the hall and knock on Topaz's door.

"I saw you. I saw you. I saw you. I saw you."

The door opened and music and a blue cloud of incense smoke came spilling out. The bracelets on Topaz's thin arm jingled from her wrist to her elbow as she reached out and wrapped her fingers around Daniel's neck, pulling him in. The door shut like a vacuum and my chanting bounced, uselessly, against the beadboard walls until I stopped.

Momma woke up around supper time. She nursed Roo and moved to her own bed and that's when I moved in with her and didn't leave for the entire winter. I lay down beside her that night and I wrapped my arms around her waist. Her nightgown was soft, blue cotton. She shivered and I pulled the covers up around her. I fell asleep with my cheek against Momma's warm back and I woke up in the morning before anyone else.

The sky was dark. There wasn't a glow from the sun or either of our two moons. I took the flashlight from beside the bed and went downstairs and sat in the big armchair in the living room. I shined the flashlight against the wall above the fireplace where my handprints had once been beside Momma's and Sol's. Elaine had hung a weaving there. It was green, like rows of corn, and its colors had once matched the Christmas greenery that was still spread, brown and dry, across the mantle. I fell asleep.

When I woke again, Elaine had covered me with a blanket. It had turned cold. I blew air out into the room and it clouded in front of my face. I pulled the blanket up tighter and listened to the sounds of Elaine and Woody moving around in the kitchen, the creak of the floor, the coffee pot hissing and perking, pans and plates clattering together. Woody crossed the kitchen and sat down at the table in my view. He took sips from his mug of coffee and started to lace his boots on. I heard the woodstove door creak open and newspaper being wadded up.

"I'll get that, Babe," Woody said. In the window behind him the sun was coming up, filling the sky with soft, pink swirls. Woody yawned.

"That's okay," I heard Elaine say. "Drink your coffee."

I could picture Elaine kneeling in front of the woodstove, her hair a knotty ponytail falling across her back, the basket of kindling beside her surrounded by wads of newspaper and a few logs of dogwood and a box of wooden matches nearby. It wasn't long before I heard the crackle of the fire and the woodstove door clanking shut.

"When will I ever learn to listen to you?" Woody said.

"It's not your fault."

The sun was up now. It hung in the sky huge and pink, washing the scene with gentle, watercolor light. It splashed pink light across my father's kitchen saint and his multi-colored floors, into Elaine's hair as she leaned over and kissed Woody and then sat down beside him.

"I guess I'll put the plastic on the windows this week." Woody leaned over to finish lacing his boots.

"I hate to see it go up," Elaine said.

"Me too. I'll get Daniel to help." Woody snorted out a grim laugh and shook his head. "I hope they leave."

Elaine put her hand on his. "I'll help with the plastic."

My mother came drifting down the stairs and went right past me without even noticing I was there. Elaine got up and pulled a chair out for her. Momma sat down. She reached down and pulled her socks up under her nightgown and hugged her old bathrobe closer to her. The blue of her nightgown shone through the worn, thin elbow of brown plaid. Elaine put a cup of coffee down in front of Momma and stood behind her, rubbing her neck. The steam swirled around the top of the mug. Woody placed his hand on Momma's.

"I just don't understand it," she said. "I've tried and tried to get him to talk to me, but he just turns a blind ear."

"A deaf ear," Woody corrected her.

"What did I say?"

"A blind ear."

Momma started laughing. "A blind ear," she said again and again. "A blind ear." She laughed and her shoulders heaved until I knew she wasn't laughing any more. She pushed the coffee away and lay her head on the table. Elaine wrapped her arms around her. Woody stroked her hand. Finally Momma lifted her head and reached behind her to touch Elaine. The blue of her nightgown flashed again through the worn material of her robe.

The sun was white now. Bright light spilled into the room. I would buy Momma a new bathrobe. I would buy a thick, heavy robe to wrap around her at night, like the arms of a man that would never leave and could always keep her warm.

Topaz and Daniel stayed the winter, hiding away in her room, and I spent the winter sleeping with Momma.

Every night I would fall asleep alone in the big iron bed and I would wake to the sound of the door latching behind her. By the dim light of the small lamp on the dresser I would watch her take all her clothes off and shiver into her nightgown and then pull on a pair of clean wool socks. She would stand beside the bed and reach behind her to untie the thong that my Uncle Jimmie's bullet was suspended from and she would lay the necklace on the table beside the bed, then quickly turn off the light and slip into bed with me. I would wrap my arms around her and try to give her my warmth.

At the first sound of the stairs creaking, we would both wake up. Momma would untangle herself from my arms and cut the electric heater on. She would pick up the Polaroid of Roo's birth night and she would sit in the rocking chair by the window turning it over and over in her hands, sometimes never even looking at it. I would lie in bed, pretending to sleep and listening to the rustlings of Daniel and Topaz down in the kitchen, stealing food and drinking beer.

One night I couldn't stand just lying there and I got up and crawled into Momma's lap. She wrapped the quilt that I had dragged off the bed around both of us.

"What are you thinking?" I asked.

The electric heater glowed and hummed at her feet. The moon was so bright that it shone in the window just like daylight and I could see the saint that Sol had drawn on the beadboard wall so many years ago. I could see it and Momma's face as clear as if the lamp had been on.

"It's been a month now," Momma said.

I didn't want to talk about Daniel. Every time Elaine asked Momma when she was going to tell Daniel and Topaz to leave, Momma changed the subject. It never seemed to help when I said that I hated him and since that was the only thing I could think of to say, I changed the subject too.

"What else do you think about?" I asked.

I felt her shoulders shrug. My ear was pressed to her chest and I could hear her heartbeat.

"I don't know," she said. "My life I guess. Your father. It was this very window I looked out of the night that you were born and he was out there shotgunning all those people."

"What else?"

Momma laughed a bitter little sound. "The choices I've made. I don't think I've made very good choices."

"What else?"

"Jimmie. I think about Jimmie."

Outside the door we heard a creak and a thud and Topaz giggling. "Shhh," someone said and then they both giggled. The door to their room opened and clicked shut again and soon we heard faint music playing.

I reached for Momma's hand and squeezed it and she said, "Jimmie wrote me a letter the week before he died. It came in the mail three weeks after the funeral. I never read it. I just held it in my hands and turned it over and over."

"I know," I said. My mother has always told me things that I already knew. "Where is it?" I asked.

The unopened letter was no longer in the box of letters

that remained in the van. Norther and Roxy and I had pawed all through that box looking for the unopened letter. It wasn't there. We opened and looked at three or four of my Uncle Jimmie's other letters but we couldn't read them. They were all in script.

"I moved it," she said. "It's in my dresser drawer." She sighed, a big sigh, like all the air escaping a balloon. "You know, if Jimmie hadn't died, you might not have ever been born."

I knew that. Norther and Roxy and I had made up a game called "dead brother." We used an old shower curtain that had been pulled from one of our woodpiles and which we had folded into a loose triangle. Norther would die and lie in the leaves and we would have a funeral. I would sit motionless on a stump and Roxy would lay the old shower curtain in my lap and I would burst into tears. Roxy and Norther would take turns dying but I never changed roles. I was always the one who was presented the shower curtain.

My mother retrieved the shower curtain from our play spot once and I held my breath as I watched her place it with the other tarps. I didn't want her to know about "dead brother" but I needn't have worried. Our sloppy triangle did not resemble a flag to her grown-up eyes.

The winter that Daniel moved down the hall was a winter full of midnight talks between my mother and myself. She would wonder out loud about all the parts of her life that she couldn't make sense of and I would listen and prod her. My mother's stories and the details of her life became a fabric that was woven into my heart. I learned, once again, about my uncle's funeral and the triangle of flag and the cold metal chairs and I learned, once again, about my father and his motorcycle and why he buried my placenta and the guest book that was signed on the night of my birth and I wondered, where was he? Was he with Jimmie?

Some nights, I didn't want to hear Momma's stories or think that I might not have ever been born, so I just stayed in bed and watched her. On the nights that the moon was a thin sliver, I could see her only by the red light of the electric heater coils. She looked ghostly and alone in the shadows of the room.

In the mornings, when I went downstairs, there would be

dirty dishes in the wash tub and empty beer cans stacked like pyramids on the table.

"This place looks like a damn frat house," Elaine said as she dragged the trash can across the floor and began to swipe the beer cans into it.

Woody sat at the table looking over the electric bill. "This bill has doubled," he said looking up to the ceiling. "They run that heater all the time."

"They're going to burn the place down if they aren't careful." Elaine dragged the trash can back.

Momma came in wearing her plaid robe with the holes in it. I hadn't bought her a new one. We hadn't been to the thrift shops lately. She poured herself a cup of coffee and sat down.

"This bill has doubled," Woody said again. "We should take that heater away from them."

"It's probably me," Momma said. "I run mine a lot too."

"Sara," Elaine scolded. "It is not you."

"Can I have some coffee?" I asked.

"You drink coffee?" Woody said.

"I used to." I was remembering the coffee I drank on the

road and how Momma fixed it for me, sweetened with sugar, blond with cream and cooled with ice cubes. "I need some coffee," I added.

Momma got up to pour me a cup. "I'll have to use honey," she told me. "We don't have any sugar." She chose the largest mug she could find and I watched her fixing it for me, dumping the honey and cream in and shucking the ice cubes out of their tray. When she set the cup in front of me she rubbed my hair and said, "You're not getting enough sleep are you?"

Every day that Norther and I came home from school, Momma would be waiting for me. If it was raining we stayed inside by the fire and played rummy. If it wasn't raining we would march off into the woods in search of honeysuckle. I helped her pull the vine out of the trees in long, chaotic strands. Then we stood there, silently untangling it and coiling it into rings that would fit inside the big aluminum pot.

I had never seen Momma weave so many baskets as she did that winter after Daniel left her. The loft of her barn was filled with them and she hung ropes from the rafters, stringing more of the smooth, blond baskets up in the air. Still she continued to weave and we continued to gather vine until we were going farther and farther from the house, deeper and deeper into the woods.

"I think you should move back upstairs," she said one day.

"Why?" I asked.

"You have circles under your eyes. You're not getting enough sleep."

"You have circles under your eyes too," I told her. "Why do you get up every night? Why don't you just stay in bed? It's warmer."

"I don't know. I just can't sleep." Momma bent her head down and clipped a piece of vine.

"You could have untangled that one, Momma. You said you wanted them long."

"I've been thinking about your father," she said. "He never cheated on me."

"Momma, he shit on the floor."

"I know. I think about that too. Do you think he would have if we'd stayed?"

"No, because you wouldn't have let him."

"Do you ever think about him?" she asked.

"Yeah."

"What do you think?" she asked.

"I don't know. He used to pay me a quarter for every joint I rolled."

Momma stopped untangling the vine and stood up straight. "He did?" She bent back to the task of untangling. "That's not right," she said.

"Well, it had to be rolled tight enough. I liked it when you came home and brought me a doughnut."

"We didn't feed you very well in those days," Momma said.

"When are you going to ask Daniel and Topaz to leave?"

"I can't ask him to leave," she said. "He was a good man until this happened."

We silently continued to unwind the vine. The only sound was the snip of our clippers until Momma suddenly said, "My brother died just before I met Sol."

I looked up at her. I couldn't believe how many times she had said this to me and how many times I had replied, "I know. You've told me."

"His tour was almost up," she said.

I nodded. Momma looked at the sky and told me a Jimmie

story. In high school, when Jimmie was a senior and she was a sophomore they used to skip class together and sneak into the woods to smoke dope and Jimmie would sometimes bring a copy of *Tom Sawyer* and read to her. Then she told me that one of Jimmie's favorite places was the graveyard in a church that was close to the school and that sometimes they would go there and Jimmie would run his fingers across the letters of a lichen-covered headstone and make up a complete life for the person buried there and that once he lay on a grave and crossed his arms across his chest.

"Why did he cross his arms?" I asked.

"It's how they lay out bodies," she told me. "Like this." She crossed her arms across her chest, clippers in one hand and a strand of vine trailing from the other. I made a note to add this to "dead brother."

"I still haven't read his letter," Momma said.

I reached over and squeezed her hand and she looked down at me.

"Why don't you read it?" I asked.

A wind came up and her hair swirled in front of her face. She smiled, but only one corner of her mouth went up. She looked older than I had ever seen her look before.

"We better get back," she said. "Elaine's keeping Roo. We'll get this stuff tomorrow." She squeezed my hand and we trudged home. At the edge of the woods, we saw Norther and Roxy standing outside the kindling barn, snapping branches and throwing them in a pile.

While Momma was downstairs helping Elaine with dinner I climbed the stairs and went into Momma's room and quietly closed the door behind me. This was the first time that I had opened Momma's dresser drawer and plunged my hand into the clothes and found Jimmie's letter. It was thick and still sealed and I held it to my heart as though I could drink it into me. That night at dinner I asked, "Where is Vietnam?"

"It's on the other side of the world," Woody said.

"Where?" I asked again.

We didn't have a map or an atlas or a globe. There was no way to point out Vietnam to me.

"Why did we fight?" I asked.

"I don't know," Woody said, shaking his head.

I had asked this question before and this was always the

answer I received and I had had enough of it.

"Well, someone must know," I said angrily and I scraped my chair across the floor and stormed upstairs to Momma's room.

I heard them murmuring below and soon I recognized Woody's footsteps on the stairs. He came in and sat in bed with me and wrapped his arms around me and I cried. "I just want to know why we were fighting and no one can tell me," I said.

"Cedar," he said. "Grown-ups don't know everything." I guess Woody tried to answer my questions. He told me about communism. I didn't want to know about communism. He told me about the American government. I didn't want to know about the American government. He told me about the draft. I didn't want to know about the draft. He told me about the moratorium. I didn't give a fig about that either. He told me about Kent State. I didn't give a damn. I wanted to know why Jimmie was dead and why my mother was so sad and why Sol and I had played "outside agitator" and why those people in Saigon wanted out and why we weren't happy when the war was over and I wanted to know who was right. I ended up as confused as anybody.

In November, Norther and I came home from school to find Elaine sitting at the kitchen table winding a skein of yarn into a ball and Momma standing at the stove poking at a pot of honeysuckle vine. The aroma filled the kitchen and steam was rising into Momma's face. I sat down on the floor to play with Baby Roo who was knocking wooden spoons against Momma's shoes. Bouncey twirled against my legs.

"They're getting up," Elaine said, raising her eyes to the creaking and muttering above us.

Roo grabbed hold of my fingers and I helped her to stand. She wobbled a few steps before whumping down onto the floor. "He never used to sleep so late," I said.

"Maybe I should have let him." Momma clamped the lid back down on the pot of vine.

The kitchen door swung open and Topaz rushed in with her hand covering her mouth. She wasn't wearing anything but boxer shorts and a tee-shirt. She rushed to the back door. "What is that awful smell?" she muffled. The door slammed behind her and we could hear her retching in the bushes.

I opened the door and hollered, "It's honeysuckle."

"Akkk," she yelled back. Momma picked Roo up and stood behind me. We watched through the screen as Topaz ran across the yard towards the outhouse.

"I'd rather vomit in the bushes," I said.

Momma shut the door and turned to look at Elaine. Elaine had stopped winding her yarn. "It's probably the drinking," she said and nodded as though to assure herself.

"Well . . ." Momma's voice trailed off and she bounced Baby Roo on her hip.

"What is it?" I asked.

"It's probably the beer," Elaine said again.

I remember the way she nodded to herself again and went back to her skein of yarn. I remember the way that Momma walked back to the stove and lifted the lid off the pot and poked at the vine again. I remember the way she lifted her head and looked out the window towards the outhouse and said once again, "Well . . ."

Two weeks later, I couldn't find Momma after school. She wasn't in the kitchen or her room. Elaine told me that she was weaving baskets. She handed me two cookies wrapped in a paper towel.

When I got to the barn where Momma worked, all I could see was the overturned tub and the wet earth spread with coils of vine. There was a half-finished basket sitting under a tree, its spokes reaching towards the sky. I turned the tub upright and scooped the vine back into it. It would take a lot of jugs of water to refill that tub and if the vine didn't soak it would turn dry and brittle. "Momma?" I creaked the barn door open and there she was, sitting on the dirt floor in the dark. "Momma, are you alright?"

"I asked them to leave," she said.

"Well, it's about time," I told her. "Do you want a cookie?"

"Do you know why I asked them to leave?"

I shook my head no, although it seemed to me like there didn't need to be any other reason.

"Topaz is pregnant," Momma told me. "He came out here to tell me. He said I should be the first to know, like I'm an aunt or something."

"When are they leaving?" I asked.

"They're not leaving. He said they don't have any money and winter's coming on and, get this, for me to have a heart. That's when I kicked the tub over and got his sneakers wet."

I pulled a leaf out of Momma's hair. "You need a bath," I said.

Momma started laughing. "You know what I told him? I told him that I rue the day I met him and Roo is the name of his child. I can't believe this." She laid her head down and started to cry and I sat in the barn patting her on the back until dusk. When we left and headed back across the yard towards the house, the windows in the kitchen glowed a tawny gold and inside I could see Elaine moving about, lifting lids off of pots and setting the table, all with one arm, while with the other one, she kept Baby Roo propped on her hip. Above the kitchen, from the window of Daniel's and Topaz's room a cold blue light shone out into the night. It was the coldest light that I have ever seen.

CHAPTER TWELVE

Daniel and Topaz did not leave. They didn't even look for somewhere else to go. They stayed and they continued their nightly kitchen raids and the construction of their beer-can pyramids. They slept late. They avoided all of us. None of us knew what stage of pregnancy Topaz was in, but whatever stage it was, they did not seem to be preparing for it at all. No midwives came to visit. No doctor's appointments seemed to be kept.

We tried not to think about it. We tried to forget about them. We tried to carry on our lives as normally as possible beneath the room with the blue light bulb. We tried to ignore them. We had breakfast and dinner as always, but when the floor creaked above us, we would look up for a moment and then at each other.

Momma never said anything more about them. She cooked and cleaned and made baskets. Elaine baked bread and helped out with Roo. Norther and I went to school.

Roxy learned a new song on the ukulele. Woody cut and stacked firewood and stapled the plastic back on the windows.

The first night the plastic was back up, it snapped and rippled and scared us all into thinking that there was someone out there. Woody turned on all the outside lights and crept around the house, carrying a stick of firewood. We stayed huddled inside. We heard Woody crunching through the leaves and then start to laugh. "It's just the plastic," he yelled. "I didn't get it stretched very tight."

We all started laughing at our relief and embarrassment and then we heard the floor creak and Topaz muttering something to Daniel. Elaine looked up. "It's nothing," she said gleefully and she grabbed my mother's hands and started to dance with her. "It's nothing to be scared of," she sang out. Momma laughed and when Woody came in she opened up her arms for him to join in. We danced ring-around-the-rosy style in the middle of the kitchen floor singing, "It's nothing. It's nothing. It's nothing." We danced until we all fell down laughing at how absurd we were acting. That's what I was laughing about anyway. Sometimes I think Momma may have been laughing at something else, laughing, finally, at how absurd her life had become. I can't be sure.

What she has said is that she doesn't know what she would have done without Elaine and Woody and me. She has said that I helped her more than I will ever know, more than I ever should have, more than any six-year-old child should ever have had to do. She has apologized to me again and again for this period of our lives, but she never did anything wrong and all that I did was continue to sleep with her in the big iron bed.

Eventually I got used to the hum of the electric heater and the rocking chair creaking back and forth and eventually I started sleeping through the night. And as winter passed, Momma must have gotten used to the creaking of the stairs as Daniel and Topaz sneaked into the kitchen. She started waking up less and less, until finally all she would do was roll over and I would wrap my arms around her and nuzzle into her flannel nightgown. The scent of my mother was soap and wood smoke and honeysuckle. The scent of my mother was everything.

One Saturday morning, I woke up to find her already

dressed and standing in front of the bureau. I snuggled under the covers and quietly watched her brush and braid her brown hair into two thick plaits. She laid the brush back down and picked up the photograph of Baby Roo's birth night. I had watched her all winter long pick this picture up and turn it over and over in her hands. One night, she had held it so close to the electric heater that I thought it might catch fire, but she was just trying to see into it and she drew it back into the darkness before it became too hot. That morning she stared deep into that other time and she traced one finger along its edge and then, very quickly, she opened the top drawer to her dresser and buried it among the clothes. She withdrew Jimmie's letter from the dresser and she held it to her lips and then turned it over in her hands and then she buried it in the clothes of her dresser also.

"I think you should move back upstairs," she said as she shut the drawer and turned towards the bed.

"How did you know I was awake?"

Momma came towards the bed and reached for the leather thong and tied it around her neck. Her hands centered the bullet so that it fell right at the hollow of her throat. When we were on the road I had watched a man finger the bullet at her throat when he was saying goodbye to her. I remember his words. "I hope I see you again," he said. I remember watching them kiss and noticing the soft way that Momma closed her eyes. I wondered if I would ever close my eyes that way.

When the bullet was centered Momma paused. "I didn't," she said. "But you are awake and I think you should move back upstairs."

Momma had asked me to move back upstairs before, but she sounded different this time. She sounded like she meant it, so instead of saying, "Momma, are you sure?" like I had been doing all winter, I just said okay.

"Roo's birthday is next week," she said. "I think we should have a party."

"Okay," I said again.

"Are you going to get up?"

I crawled out of bed with the blanket wrapped around me.

"It's warm," Momma said and she reached out and tried to yank the blanket away from me. I held on and in the holding on she pulled me to her and hugged me. Momma ran her hand across my head and her callouses snagged in my hair.

"Is it really warm?" I asked testing the air with my breath. It made no cloud.

Roo started crying from her crib and Momma went to her, cooing comfort in her ear as she picked her up.

"Momma can we have ice cream at Roo's party?"

"We'll see."

I reached under the bed for the bucket to pee in.

"Go use the outhouse," Momma said. "It's warmer out there than it is in here." I padded downstairs in my bare feet. Momma was right. Outside, the air was balmy and soft. The ground was cold on my feet. I looked closely at the dogwood tree next to the outhouse but I couldn't see buds. It looked as empty as it had all winter, but somehow I knew that something was stirring deep inside of it, just as something had stirred deep inside of Momma after the long cold winter.

Back inside the house, Elaine had opened all the doors.

"I wish I could open the windows," she said. "But I don't dare take that plastic off."

Instead, she built a small crackling fire to take the night

chill off. By mid-afternoon, the house was warm and sunny and the scent of the morning fire had been replaced with clean, fresh air. I spent the day helping Momma gather vine.

"You really don't have to help me," she said.

"I don't mind."

"You could be playing."

"I don't mind, Momma."

"Last time," she said and from the way she said it, I knew it would be.

After dinner, I went upstairs and dressed in my nightgown. Norther and Roxy were still downstairs and the attic room was filled with soft muffled voices from down deep in the kitchen. I ran my hand along the wood of the slanted ceiling and picked at a piece of rosin that oozed out of a knot over my bed. I looked at every single painting that I had leaning against the knee wall. I hardly recognized them. It had been so long since I had been in the attic that it felt like a strange place, a place where I had lived as a child.

"You're back?" Norther asked from behind me.

I hadn't heard him come up the stairs.

I nodded. "Momma says so."

"I missed you." He came over and sat on my bed. "Woody fixed the leak," he said. "We moved your bed back."

I sat beside him.

"I missed you," he said again and he wrapped his arms around me.

That night, Norther and Roxy tucked me in and they covered my blanket with all the magical items they could think of that I could sleep with, evergreen boughs and pine needles and special buttons and rocks.

"To keep you here," Roxy said. She had given up the ukulele and was making her own magic now.

For the entire week, it was warm every day and cool every night. In the mornings, Elaine built the fire up and in the afternoons she opened the doors to let the air in and pondered out loud when to take the plastic off the windows.

Three days before her first birthday, Roo took off talking. "Oxy," she'd say when Roxy picked her up. "Eeder," she said to me. The only name that she said perfectly was Momma. She learned other words too. "Eat," she screamed at the table. "Pot," she would say, banging a spoon against an old kettle. "Pot," she would say again, as she climbed up on her stubby legs and lunged herself towards Woody, while he sat at the table rolling a joint.

On Saturday morning, I watched Momma balance on the aluminum ladder that was propped against the big oak tree in front of the house. She was stringing paper lanterns up in the branches for Roo's birthday party. They bobbed in the breeze, blue, green, yellow, red. When she climbed down she said, "I may as well take this ladder out into the woods while I've got it."

"For what?" I asked.

"Wisteria," she said. "I'm going to try to weave with it."

"Do you need help?"

"No, Cedar. Go play," she told me. I watched her walk away carrying the big clippers in one hand and the ladder under her other arm. "See if Elaine needs help," she hollered over her shoulder.

I ran to the house. The kitchen smelled like chocolate and Elaine shooed me outside with threats of what she would do to me if the cake fell. I had the whole day ahead of me. I spent part of it gathering kindling with Norther and Roxy. When that was done, we walked down to the pond we had tried to build. Roxy measured its depth with a stick.

"It's deeper," she reported. "I'm sure of it."

"I want to paint," I said suddenly. "I want to go upstairs and paint."

And that's what I did. I painted three pictures that day and I would have painted more, if not for Roo's birthday party and the fact that I ran out of cardboard and most of my paints had frozen over the winter and when I squeezed the tubes, only a watery stream of color would come out. From the window I saw Momma coming out of the woods with a completed basket made of thick brown vine. I heard the door to the kitchen slam and her calling my name and then climbing the stairs. She handed me the heavy brown basket.

"This is for you," she said. "I thought you could put your socks in it."

"You didn't have to boil the vine?" I asked.

"Not with wisteria." Momma leaned over me and admired my paintings.

"My paints got frozen," I said. "They're no good any more."

"I'll buy you some new ones." She rubbed my head and

again I could feel the callouses on her hands gently tugging in my hair. "It's time for Roo's party," she said. "Remind me to get the ladder out of the woods before dark."

The picnic table was set up beneath the paper-lanterned tree. It was draped with an old sheet and in the center of it were a plate of sandwiches, a big bowl of potato salad, and a shiny chocolate cake with one slim birthday candle jammed into the center of it. We admired it while eating our lunch and then while taking turns cranking the handle of the ice cream maker. I had just gotten up from the bench after my turn at cranking and Norther had just sat down for his when we heard the screen door slamming.

Topaz and Daniel were on the front steps. We had barely seen either of them since Daniel had announced Topaz's pregnancy to Momma. Topaz's stomach was swollen. Her face and ankles were puffy and her feet swelled out over a pair of moccasins. In her hands she carried her blue suede boots. Maybe she was six months along. Maybe seven. None of us knew. Daniel's beard had grown out and was no longer neatly trimmed. It sagged down his chest in a mass of wiry black hair. He was carrying the battered blue suitcase that

Topaz had arrived with and he took her arm and helped her down the steps and across the yard to his car. He opened the passenger door for her and then went around to the driver's side. Neither of them said anything to us and we didn't say anything to them, but I swear the birds stopped singing and Roo stopped banging her spoon against the high chair and the breeze became as still and quiet as the air in a tomb.

I walked over to Momma and very gently placed my hand on her shoulder. She reached up and touched my fingers. The old Falcon cranked up and bumped out of sight. We listened to it wind around the curves and speed up through the big puddles and slow down for the gullies. At the bottom of the hill, it hit the blacktop and revved its way out of earshot and it became quieter than I had ever known it to be at Two Moons. It was a stillness that I have only felt that once and then the breeze picked up again and above me I could hear the crinkle of the paper lanterns and the birds starting to sing. The handle of the ice cream maker creaked into motion. Roo started giggling and throwing crumbs in Norther's hair. Elaine playfully slapped Woody's hand away as he snitched a finger full of icing off the cake. Momma patted my hand and we piled the presents in front of Roo.

We were packing things up when the Falcon returned and Daniel got out alone. He walked to the front porch steps and then abruptly turned around and walked towards us. Momma picked Roo up and held her.

"Is there any cake left?" Daniel asked.

"In the kitchen," someone said.

Daniel faced Momma. He reached out and tickled Roo under her chin. I could feel Momma's body going stiff and freezing up next to me.

"I thought you should know," Daniel said, "that Topaz is gone. It's over, Sara. I'm sorry."

Momma shifted Roo to her other arm, away from Daniel's tickling fingers. "You don't think it all goes back to the way it was, do you?"

"I know I made a mistake," he said, looking down at the ground.

"She's carrying your child," Momma said and she marched past him towards the house.

I ran after her and slipped my hand into hers. "Do you want me to sleep with you tonight?" I asked.

"I'll be fine, Cedar," she said. "I can look after myself."

I wasn't so sure. I stayed by her the rest of the afternoon, sitting on the kitchen floor, playing with Roo while Momma and Elaine prepared dinner. Norther and Roxy begged me to come outside but I didn't. And when Daniel came downstairs and tried once again to talk to Momma, I was right there in the way. But maybe I didn't need to worry so much.

"Fuck you," she told him.

"Just talk to me," he begged.

"Like you talked to me?" she asked.

"It'll take time," he said. "I'm going out for some beer. Do you need anything?"

"Fuck you," Momma said again.

It turned cold again that night. We built a fire as soon as the sun set, but that's not what burned the house down. Sometimes I think it was passion that burned the house down, but that's not what the report from the fire department said.

The report from the fire department said, "The fire originated in one bedroom, probably a lit cigarette dropped on the mattress."

Daniel did not return until late that night. I had already drifted to sleep but the car lights circling the attic room woke me up and I lay in bed listening to the angry voices of Daniel and my mother. I lay in bed and swore to myself that if I heard the sounds of lovemaking, I would get up. But I never heard that and the argument was still going on when I finally drifted off to sleep.

When I woke up again, it was to the screaming of my name. My throat was dry and raw and a thick gray smoke was rolling up the stairs into the attic. I yelled for Momma, but it was Woody's arms that wrapped around me. I was in his arms with Roxy. She was coughing. Norther was running down the stairs in front of us. I could hear his feet slapping down the steps. I could hear Woody urging him on. In the hallway, there was a bright wall of flame coming from Daniel's room and I could see Momma trapped outside of her room, the fire roaring between her and the staircase. I could hear Roo wailing in her arms. I screamed for her and struggled to get loose, but Woody was holding me tight.

"Jump onto the porch roof," he yelled. "Sara, jump onto the porch roof."

She ran back and forth in the small hallway. The cage of fire roared like a train. A piece of the staircase fell in. I screamed and screamed. "Momma. Momma. Momma."

Woody passed Roxy and me to Elaine and then ran back into the house. I struggled to get loose, but Elaine held tight and carried me out into the yard by the picnic table still draped with the old sheet. I remember kicking against her, but she held me so tight that I was hardly moving. I remember Norther with his arms wrapped around Roxy. She buried her face into his body. I remember the moment that the flames thrashed through the roof of the house. I remember seeing the plastic on one of the windows melting and dripping down in bright red dots. Woody burst out of the house and went running towards the barn. Elaine's arms were skin-tight around me.

"She's on the roof," Norther yelled. I stopped struggling and through the smoke I could see Momma, with Baby Roo in her arms, standing at the edge of the porch roof. Her nightgown billowed against her legs. Behind her the fire was spreading across the roof of Two Moons. Woody came running back from the barn, empty-handed.

"Oh, God," Elaine said. "Where the fuck is the ladder?" She lowered me to the ground and shook my shoulders. "You have to stay here," she said. "You have to stay here." She let go of me and ran towards the house. Norther reached out and put his other arm around me.

Woody was up on the railing now. Elaine was right behind him. He held onto one of the porch posts and reached up, just barely above the overhang. Momma knelt down at the edge of the roof. She kissed Roo once and passed her to Woody's groping hand. Woody grabbed Roo by the collar and swung her over the edge and into Elaine's waiting arms. Elaine backed away from the house, but she did not leave. I could see that she was bouncing Roo on her shoulder and sometimes looking her over to see that she was all right and sometimes looking up and watching Momma as she lay down on the porch roof and backed herself over the edge. Woody wrapped his arms around her dangling legs. The glass of one upstairs window exploded and my mother and Woody came tumbling down to the ground. No sooner had they hit the ground than they were up running, with Woody slowing down just long enough to grab Elaine's arm.

When Momma got to us, her arms went straight around me. Her body was warm from the fire. Her nightgown was singed to a smoky gray. I nuzzled my face into her neck. She smelled like burnt hair and had never smelled so good to me. She pulled away and held me at arm's length, inspecting my face, rubbing her fingers over my eyebrows, asking again and again if I was okay. Her own eyebrows were wiry burnt curls and her hair was frizzed on the ends and her face was streaked with soot.

"Where's Daniel?" Woody asked.

No one knew where Daniel was and as Woody asked the question the roof of the house caved in and flames leapt out the open front door. We backed away and stood at the top of the driveway. Momma ran back to the picnic table and got the old sheet and wrapped it around Roo. Behind us, we could hear the wail of sirens coming our way.

By the time the fire trucks had labored up the driveway, our house was smoldering rubble with a sunrise behind it. I remember steam rising into the pink air and the silhouettes of the firemen as they searched through the rubble. I remember the red lights of the fire truck flashing across the trees and our faces. I remember the shout of discovery. I remember watching Daniel's body being lifted out of the debris and laid on the ground.

CHAPTER THIRTEEN

We spent that night in the pottery barn. The next day, the minister of the Baptist Church down the road brought us blankets and clothes. The minister got his shiny gray car stuck in the spring puddles and Woody had to help push him out. Norther and Elaine and I walked down there with them. Woody pushed and pushed while the minister tried to rock the car out but finally Woody told him that he was going to have get out and push too and Elaine got in the driver's seat. I remember the spray of mud spattered across the minister's gray pants legs, pants made from a material that was nearly as shiny as his car had been before he drove up our driveway. I remember six boxes lined up in the pine needles on the bank of our driveway. They contained clothes and blankets and flashlights with fresh batteries and dishes and a Bible. When the minister finally got his car unstuck, he shook Woody's hand and said, "Thank you, brother. Come worship with us." But he never ventured up the driveway again. Our sorry souls were too much trouble to try and save.

Two days after the fire, Bouncey the cat showed up, mewing at the pottery barn door. Her fur was a sooty gray and her whiskers were gone. When she rubbed against Roo, she left a black streak across her tee-shirt. Elaine poured her a saucer of milk from the cooler outside the door. Bouncey lapped up three saucers full, then settled in the sun to bathe herself.

Three days after the fire, Daniel's body was shipped to Michigan, to the town that he had grown up in, the town where his mother and father and brother still lived. All that we could do was hold a private ceremony beside the placenta grave, a ceremony in which each of us intended to say something, but none of us did. We stood there silently, the breeze lifting the scent of Two Moons towards us. No longer the scent of cookies and bread and wood smoke and pot, it was now the scent of wreckage.

Finally Elaine spoke. "Well, perhaps we don't have anything to say right now."

We nodded and drifted away, Woody and Elaine heading

towards the pottery barn where they were packing Woody's tools and wheel. They had decided to move to the mountains and they begged Momma to go with them, swearing we would find a house and start over, swearing we would get it right this time.

Momma said no. She didn't know what we'd do and as we drifted away from the placenta grave that day I said, "Please, Momma. Let's go with Woody and Elaine. Please."

She shifted Roo from one hip to another, but all she said was, "We should have had that preacher. Someone who didn't know him." She sat on the bumper of the van and looked towards the house, bouncing Roo on her knee. Her hand lifted to her throat, searching for the bullet that would never hang there again. I sat beside her and watched Woody and Norther load the pottery wheel into the bed of the truck.

"Peez," Roo said. "Peez."

Elaine came out of the barn carrying blankets. She shook them out and the dust glistened in the air around her before settling onto the ground. She draped the blankets across some bushes to air out in the sun and then she came towards us, her feet clopping across the ground in her donated loafers. "Are you sure you won't come with us?" she asked.

I looked at Momma pleadingly, but she paid no attention to me. She shook her head no, for the hundredth time. She stood and hiked her pants up. They were bunched together at the waist and held tight with a diaper pin.

"Peez," Roo said again, echoing what I had been saying for three days now.

"What will you do?" Elaine asked.

"I don't know," Momma answered.

"There's no point in staying here," Elaine said.

"I have to wait for Daniel's brother. He's coming for the car next week." Momma sat back down.

That afternoon, we stood at the top of the driveway, me holding Baby Roo and Momma clutching the fifty dollars that Woody had given her and we watched the old red truck lump down the driveway for the last time. Roxy leaned out the window and waved. Norther sat in the back, close to the tailgate. His brown hair blew in his face. I lifted my hand to wave at the same time he did and then they rounded the curve out of sight.

As always, I could track where the truck was by the sounds

of the engine. Through the puddles, around another big curve, straddling the gullies and onto the pavement, speeding off towards the highway and across the Haw River. I knew the exact moment that they were truly gone. Momma and I stood there like statues in the wax museums we used to visit.

That night, I dreamed about them. I dreamed that I was in the kitchen watching Elaine rub Woody's back. I dreamed that I was in my bed in the attic and I could hear them making love. I dreamed that Norther and Roxy were covering my bed with pine boughs and fall leaves. I dreamed that I heard the sound of Woody's axe falling through firewood. I dreamed that somewhere in the rubble of Two Moons I found the crystal that Norther had given me and I held it to my heart once again.

We lived for five more days in the pottery barn. We fixed it up as best we could, spreading our donated blankets on the ground like a bed. The blankets were all lime green or bright orange, with fuzzballs, but they would do, Momma said. We sorted through the clothes left to us, making four piles, one for each of us and one that none of us would ever wear, no matter how desperate we were. It came down to one box each and Momma lined them up against one wall of the pottery barn. The rest of the clothes we used as padding beneath our bed. We hauled wood from the stack left near the house to just outside our door. I got two of Momma's baskets from her barn. One I filled with kindling and the other I filled with the torn up boxes and all the paper I could find in our van, except for Jimmie's letters. When Momma found the Bible in this basket, she took it out and laid it beside our bedroll.

"I can't burn this," she said.

"The paper's too thin," I agreed.

"It's not that," she said. "I just can't burn the Bible."

The next morning, Momma was plowing through the van looking for something. "Do you have a pen?" she asked me.

"I don't have anything," I told her.

"I need a pen. I want to label those boxes. Every time I'm looking for something for Roo, I reach into the wrong box."

"You could use some charcoal from the house," I suggested.

Momma looked up the hill towards the blackened hull. "I can't go up there," she said. "I just need a pen." She continued to plow through the van.

"Maybe there's one in Daniel's car."

"I can't look in there either."

"I'll look," I told her.

I went to Daniel's old Falcon and opened the door. The floor was littered with candy wrappers and soda cans and quart beer bottles. I found an old sketch pad in the back seat but it was filled already with Daniel's doodlings, mostly sketches of my mother during our trip back to North Carolina. There was a piece of paper in the glove box with Topaz's name and an address written in below it. I left it there. I found his wallet, the leather worn to a shine from riding in his back pocket. I fingered his driver's license, still New Mexico, never switched over to North Carolina. I stared into his eyes and tried to feel something like forgiveness, but I don't think I felt it. I put the license back and three photographs fell out, all of them black and white. One was a picture of my mother and me standing on the highway beside a sign that said in white script letters, "Welcome to North Carolina." Another picture was of Topaz, sitting on the front porch of Two Moons. The last one was a woman that I barely recognized, Leah from the photographs on the adobe walls in New Mexico, the woman that Daniel left to be with Momma. She stood beside a tall saguaro cactus. It reached its arms towards the sky like a TV preacher. I put these back. There was a ten-dollar bill and I took that, cramming it into the pocket of my jeans. There was no pen that I could find and I looked up and saw that Momma was standing beside our van, waiting for one, like finding a pen had become the focus of her life, an item crucial to our survival, getting the boxes of clothes labeled was all that mattered.

"I'll get you some charcoal," I yelled and I trudged up the hill towards what was left of Two Moons.

I had visited the house before. Norther and I had circled it while it was still steaming, but I had not visited since it had cooled off. It had been hulking up above us on the hill, but I had just looked at it, like the body of a relative laid out in the living room.

Our possessions were strewn across the black, sooty rubble like artifacts from a ghost town. Woody's old felt hat with the brim burned off lay beside a piece of Elaine's yellow bread bowl. One of Roxy's slippers had crayons and the bright purple tube of a bong melted to it. The back porch was not completely burned and the floorboards were stripes of hard, brittle bubbles in different colors. One of my paintings lay oddly propped against the remains of the doorframe, as though set there by a human hand. I picked it up, a painting of our outhouse with Daniel and a pregnant Momma standing outside. A smear of soot ran across it, just like the brown smear my father had left across our handprints over the mantel. I dropped it back into the rubble.

I was looking into our kitchen. The woodstove was turned over and pinned beneath a large, black beam. I cracked a piece of charcoal off for Momma and turned to walk away but something called me back, called my eyes back to rake the wrecked kitchen, daring them to find it. It was like the thump of a huge heart. It was like the thump of Two Moons. The thump of my whole life. There were pots and pans scattered among broken dishes and a sprinkling of blackened Scrabble tiles. The telephone was a snarl of green plastic stuck to one piece of the beadboard wall and beside it was a piece of the saint my father had drawn. It was the saint's hands that remained, holding the frog cupped in their palms. I wanted it. Without thought to danger or dirt, I climbed into the rubble and claimed it, snapping it back and forth off of the larger piece of wood until it broke.

Momma didn't say a thing about it when I returned to the pottery barn filthy with soot. She took the charcoal from me and labeled our boxes. She eyed the saint's hands holding the frog as I set it carefully against the wall and she said, "Go down to the creek and wash off."

It was the same day that Daniel's brother, David, arrived. They could have been twins or it could have been Daniel's ghost walking up the driveway and across the yard towards us. We stood at the door of the barn and watched. He had the same gait, the same dark, glittery eyes and full red lips showing through the same black beard.

"I've come for the car," he said to Momma. It was the same voice that had wooed her two years before.

"The keys are in it," she replied.

Roo reached out towards him but she didn't say anything. She didn't know the word for Daddy or even Daniel.

David turned and walked away. He opened the door to the Falcon and then stood still, staring towards the house where his brother had died. Then he got in and started the car and left. I prayed for him not to get stuck in the puddles. He didn't and he was gone as quickly as he had come and he was never introduced to his niece.

I have never known what Daniel told his family about Momma and me and Roo and Topaz. I have never known if they knew that he had a child or—if things went well with Topaz—children. And as odd as it may sound, as much as I disliked the woman, I have wondered about her and her baby. I have wondered if it was a boy or a girl and what she named it. I have looked at my half sister, Roo, and thought to myself, somewhere in this world, Roo has another half sibling and, somewhere in this world, I have a father named Albert Masey who called himself Sol and drew saints on beadboard walls. Somewhere in the world, these people live and breathe, but it's been hard to think of them as real. It's been hard to think of any people, besides my mother, as anything besides transient, but she may have been the most transient of all.

When we heard Daniel's brother burning rubber on the pavement, Momma said, "We're leaving."

CHAPTER FOURTEEN

Just like that, we left Two Moons. Momma dumped her clothes into the bed of the van and used her box to cram Bouncey the cat into. Bouncey reached out of the crack in the folded down top and frantically pawed the air. She meowed miserably while I stood balanced in the back of the van and watched Two Moons disappear.

Outside of Chapel Hill, Bouncey broke free and started roaming the van, pitifully calling to the other cars that passed by. I tried to hold her in my lap, but she clawed at me until I let her go. We let her roam. It was my job to keep her away from Momma while she drove and it kept me occupied all the way through North Carolina. Just inside of the South Carolina border, Bouncey settled down. She stretched herself across the dashboard and watched the road, like it was something she had been doing all her life.

"Where are we going?" I asked.

"To your grandparents' house," Momma said. "In Atlanta, Georgia."

Momma no longer seemed to be in the trance that had carried her through the last few days. She was acting decisively and I guess she felt good about that.

I was less sure. I had never met my grandparents.

We drove through the night, stopping for gas three times and food once. At Stuckey's Momma called her parents collect and let them know we were coming. When she slid back into the booth she smiled and said, "Your grandmother sure is a God-fearing woman. She's upset that you're illegitimate, but she'll warm up to you."

"What does illegitimate mean?" I asked.

"It means you were born without a father."

"I have a father. Sol is my father. He . . ."

I was going to say, "He buried my placenta. He drew on the walls. He taught me how to roll joints," but Momma didn't let me finish.

She clasped her hand over her mouth and said, "God, I can't believe I said that. I cannot believe I said that." She took her hand away and said, "I'm sorry, Cedar. What I meant to say is that illegitimate is a child born to a woman who is not married."

"Like Roo and me?"

"Yes, like you and Roo."

"Why does it have a name like that, Momma? No one can tell just by looking at us."

"It's stupid," Momma said. "I'm sorry I brought it up. Forget about it."

But I couldn't forget about it. "Momma, if Jimmie had been married and his wife had gotten pregnant and then he died in the war before the baby was born, does that make it illegitimate?"

"No," she said. "That's even more tragic."

"More tragic than what?"

"Than being born without a father."

"I have a father," I said again, but Momma was silent.

We stopped to sleep at a rest stop just outside of Atlanta and it meant that we arrived just in time for breakfast. Gramma was not nearly as scary as I had expected. In fact, she wasn't scary at all. She wrapped her arms around me and gave me a big hug. She was softer than anyone I had ever felt and she smelled like cinnamon. Her hair was a short, cropped gray, with a very unnecessary hair net plopped on top and her apron was dusty with flour. Inside the house, she offered us cinnamon rolls with butter. When I asked for coffee, she gave me milk.

Grandpa was thin and frail and his skin hung loosely off his bones. He dared me to fish a stick of chewing gum out of his pocket and he insisted I call him Paw-Paw, which is what Momma had called his father.

The house was low and made of brick. It spread itself across a surreally green lawn and was surrounded by boxwood bushes that had been whipped into submission by Paw-Paw's electric hedgers. The boxwoods grew more plumb and level than any of the walls of Two Moons.

I wanted Paw-Paw to build me a playhouse with them, a small green room with a window chopped out and a stretch of canvas for a roof. I mapped it out on the lawn once and showed it to him. He liked the idea, but Gramma did not. If not for Gramma, Paw-Paw could probably have been talked into anything.

Years later, at the School of the Arts in Winston-Salem, I

made my own little house of boxwood bushes. I used Paw-Paw's electric hedgers that I had inherited. I cut out windows that were shaped like those of a cathedral and I inserted frames of colored paper. The roof was white canvas rolled across pieces of still-green bamboo. The project earned me an A+, and later, a career making boxwood playhouses for the children of wealthy parents who lived in houses so unlike Two Moons that I would almost do the work for free, just so the child could have something that was a little bit small and green and different.

At Gramma's and Paw-Paw's house, I got my own room. It was Uncle Jimmie's room once and the fat triangle of flag that my mother had told me about sat on the edge of the dresser. When Gramma showed me the room, she picked up the flag and tucked it onto the top shelf of the closet.

"Now, Cedar," Gramma said. "I know this looks like a boy's room, but you can decorate it any way you want. It's your room now."

"Thank you," I mumbled. I was looking at the dark plaid bedspreads that covered the twin maple beds, the matching curtains that were drawn tight, the brown carpet, the few square bottles of aftershave lined in front of the mirror next to a framed picture of a woman with long blond hair that flipped up at the ends.

Behind me I could hear my mother saying, "Mom, we really won't be staying that long."

"Is this you?" I asked, pointing to the picture.

"No. That's Cynthia," my mother said. "She was Jimmie's girlfriend."

"Fiancée," my grandmother corrected.

"What's a fiancée?"

"A person who's engaged to be married," Momma told me.

"I suppose we should pack all this stuff away," Gramma said. She walked over to the dresser and picked the picture up in her soft hands. She started to gather the aftershave bottles.

"You can leave it." I touched her hand. "It's okay for now."

Gramma said, "Well, we can deal with it later, I suppose." She lined everything up exactly the way it was. She placed the picture carefully back onto the polished surface of the dresser, angling it just the way that it had been before. I could tell that it was a motion she had done a thousand times since Jimmie's death, maybe even a thousand times in one day. "I think they would have made us some beautiful grandchildren," she said.

"You have beautiful grandchildren," my mother told her in a voice that had an edge to it.

"Oh, of course I do." Gramma looked down at me.

I may not have looked like much. I was wearing cast-off clothes that didn't fit me well. The pants were too big and the tee-shirt was too small and I was dirty. Gramma rubbed my head. "We've got to go shopping for you," she said. "What a terrible thing." She turned away, shaking her head. I don't know if she was thinking of the fire or Uncle Jimmie or maybe just my appearance. I learned that I could never tell what Gramma was really thinking.

Momma told me later that it was that way for her too and after Gramma left the room that day still shaking her head and talking about a "terrible thing," Momma stayed, leaning in the doorway. "Are you going to be all right here?" she asked.

I nodded.

"It won't be for long," she said. "We've just got to get some money together and then we'll leave."

"Okay," I agreed.

"Don't draw on the walls," she instructed me. Her eyes opened menacingly wide. She needn't have said it. I could tell that these were walls you didn't draw on.

We must have stayed longer than Momma had intended, because I lived in my dead uncle's room for two years and eventually Roo moved in with me. I never took any of Uncle Jimmie's things away and as I accumulated my own possessions I fitted them around his. Sometimes I would pull the desk chair over to the closet and I would get the triangle of flag down from the top shelf. I would sit on one of the dark plaid bedspreads and I would hold it in my lap, the same way that Gramma had done at Jimmie's funeral, the year that my mother met my father. I would think about Two Moons and sleeping with Momma that winter and the way she would shake her head and say, "You might not have ever been born." I would remember the bullet on its snake of leather, coiled on the table next to the bed. I would remember Jimmie's unopened letter in my mother's hands. I would remember the glow and hum of the electric heater. I would remember the story of my birth and the way Momma would point down to the placenta grave on a full-mooned night and say, "It was right down there," and if I looked I could almost see Sol dancing around a fire, shotgunning people with one of his perfectly rolled joints, the yard behind him a dim sea of cars.

In Jimmie's room, I would touch the stiff surface of the flag. I wanted to unfold it and see if I could fold it back. It was nothing like our triangle of shower curtain when we had played "dead brother." I wanted to spread Jimmie's flag across the ugly plaid bedspread and crawl under it.

My mother slept in her old room, across the hall from me. The bedspreads on her twin beds were white with pink poodles appliqued on them. Behind the mirror over her dresser, my mother's pompons trailed their high school colors, blue and white, down the wall. Pinned above one of the beds was a poster of the Beatles, before they grew beards and shoulder-length hair, nothing like the pictures from the White Album that we had left stapled to the walls of our outhouse. Taped to my mother's dresser mirror was a photograph of Jimmie. He was wearing fatigues and boots. His dog tags hung down his naked and hairless chest. He was grinning and standing in front of an overturned jeep. He had dimples. He held two fingers up in a "V." His hair was not a shaved military cut but instead was a mop of curly blond. The land behind him was flat and green and the sky was flat and blue.

"Did you ever read his letter?" I asked one day while fingering this picture.

"I never did," Momma said. She was sitting on the bed, clipping price tags off of new clothes.

"Do you wish you had?"

"I wish it hadn't burned," she said. She started to put the clothes on hangers. "Tomorrow I go looking for a job."

"In these?" I asked holding up the gray skirt and the black shoes with the tiny heels.

"Yes, in these." She snatched them away from me.

"Can you walk in them?"

"Of course I can."

"Prove it."

Momma sighed. She kicked off her sneakers and slipped the little shoes on and went clipping across the floor. Her ankle twisted only once.

"Pretty good," I said. "You been practicing?"

"I have to get a job, Cedar."

With these clothes and pantyhose that miraculously did not run during her interview, my mother landed a job as a secretary in a law firm. She worked eight hours a day, five days a week. She built up her wardrobe and saved her money and tried to find an apartment that we could afford but she could never make it work. Her salary would not cover rent and utilities and food for three and childcare. For nearly a year, she looked for a place, reading the ads and driving the old van out to look every weekend, but every Monday found us still at the low brick house with the green lawn. And meanwhile, I had started eating hamburgers and watching TV.

One Saturday afternoon, Momma and I had been riding around Atlanta visiting apartments. The ones we could afford were grimy and dark. There was no point in looking at the ones we couldn't afford. Roo was staying with Gramma and Momma and I had been out looking all day. Momma bought us sandwiches and Cokes for lunch and we went to a park to eat. I was eight years old. We settled at a picnic table and spread our lunch out. Momma's hair was blowing in her face and she expertly wrapped it up at the base of her neck. It would stay that way long enough for her to eat. I had seen her do this before. I was just opening my potato chips when a man walked by. His long dark hair whipped in the breeze behind him. He smiled at Momma and nodded hello.

"Who was that?" I asked, even though I knew they were strangers. All my life, I had seen men smiling at Momma this way.

"I don't know," she said. Her eyes were following his slim frame as he walked down the hill. I tried to see what she was seeing, but whatever she saw in those blue-jean-clad hips eluded me. Momma sighed. "I miss touch," she said. I placed my hand on hers. She looked down and smiled at me, but she shook her head no. "I miss a man's touch," she said, letting me know, for the very first time, that there was something I could not do for her.

We had been living with Gramma and Paw-Paw for a year now. The places that we looked at to live were all apartments, units crammed next to units, kitchens without windows over the sink, some without windows at all. The closest I could feel to Two Moons was beside the creek that ran behind the brick ranch house and after school I would go sit on its banks, tossing rocks in it or sketching or just lying back with my eyes closed. One day, I made a sailboat like the one that Jimmie had made for Momma and I set it in the water and watched it dive into the current and turn over. Its paper towel sail slipped off the pencil mast and became a disintegrating blob of sog. Gramma never bought the best brands of anything.

Roo was two years old. She was walking and talking and something inside of me hurt for her. She would never get to draw on the walls. Her floors would always be level and the same color. Her baths would always be deep and warm. I wanted her to know sponge baths and gallon jugs of water clustered behind a woodstove and the chill of a morning run to the outhouse, because along with these things came the silent swoop of an owl after a mouse, the comforting snap of plastic covering drafty windows, the radiant warmth of a well-built fire.

Momma started dating a lawyer at her office, a man named Jack. I think that Momma was as unfamiliar with dating as I was. For a year, they went out together. Maybe they made love somewhere else, but I never knew about it. She was always home and sleeping alone under the pink poodle bedspread the next morning.

Jack was skinny and clean-shaven. I grew to like him after they were married, but he was so unlike any man I had ever known that he didn't seem like a man at all. He was steady and predictable and probably just what we needed. He moved us to Richmond, Virginia, and he paid for private schooling for Roo and myself and we never wanted for anything again.

Roo and I were in the wedding. We wore pink dresses with stiff white petticoats. Momma wore a billowing white cloud of a dress. Gramma cried. The wedding cake was tall and sweet, with a candy gavel on top.

It was the last time I ever saw Norther and Roxy and Woody and Elaine. Woody danced with me standing on his shoes, the same way that we had danced across the kitchen floor of Two Moons. They had found a house in the mountains. Elaine told me that it was huge, an old abandoned mansion with twelve-foot-high ceilings and strange noises in the attic. They called it Toad Hall and they lived in it with several other people. Norther said it was cold and that even Elaine's perfectly built fires could not warm it up.

He told me this out in the graveyard of the church. We had sneaked away and sank down together behind the largest tombstone. We held hands and this was all that he said. As for me, I said nothing, but I know we sat there for at least an hour, just feeling our fingers intertwined.

I will say this for Jack. He moved us to a house, not an apartment. Our house had a window over the sink and that was important to Momma. The window looked out into a deep jungled yard with a gazebo at its center.

I will also say this for Jack. His love and care for Momma and us was unwavering and he was a damn good cook, given a barbecue pit.

He set up his law practice, with Momma as his secretary. I was enrolled in a private Quaker school, although none of us were Quaker. When Roo turned six, she was enrolled in the same school and she insisted that her teachers and classmates and me, if I could please remember, call her Pat, short for Patina. At home, she remained Roo.

Momma and Jack did not have children of their own. Evidently we were enough. At night, I listened for the sounds of lovemaking, sounds that had become so familiar to me at Two Moons. I did not often hear it. What I did hear was gentle murmuring, calm and soothing discussions about the office or a case that Jack had taken or where to go for the holidays.

I settled into the safety of this world without knowing it was safe. We had a house with a thermostat on the wall and vents in every room. With a flick of your finger, there was heat. We had hot and cold running water and a stainless steel sink and an indoor toilet that was cleaned by a woman who came weekly. We had an automatic dishwasher and a freezer full of meat and cars that ran. We did not have a creek to dam up or puddles to fishtail through or a night sky filled with glittering stars. Our walls were white and clean and our floors were level.

I could see that Momma was trying to forget about the past. The stories stopped. She tried to move on, into the next phase of her life, but some things did not change. Jimmie's box of letters remained in the van that remained in the driveway.

When I was eleven years old, John Lennon died. Momma insisted that they close up the office and Jack complied. They came and got me out of school and, once home, they paid the babysitter. Roo was five years old. Jack stayed in the house with her, but Momma and I went out to the old van. We lay down in the pile of clothes that still covered the floor and Momma cried and I held her. At eight o'clock, Jack brought us sandwiches and blankets and a flashlight and then left us alone. Momma and I spent the night of December 8, 1980, nestled together in the back of the VW van that my father had bought for my birth. The clothes that had been tossed into the back on the day that we left Two Moons left a smoky smell in the interior and I woke up often during the night as did Momma. She talked, just like she had during that last winter in North Carolina. She talked about all the same things. She told me stories about Two Moons and my father and Daniel and by the light of the flashlight she read me parts of Jimmie's letters. I had read them all one day before Momma came home from work but in Momma's voice, her face slightly illuminated by the light of the flash-light, I heard Jimmie's voice.

"The leeches are as big as snails. We had five KIA and ten wounded."

I heard mortar fire. I heard screams. I heard the names of

nearly 60,000 people on a wall that was not built yet. And he signed every one of them with a countdown of his time left.

"Two months down and ten to go, Love Jimmie."

"Six months left, Love Jimmie."

"Only twelve weeks left, Sara, and I'll be stateside."

When I was sixteen, my mother finally sold the VW van. I removed my father's lime-green bandanna that was still tied around the gear shift and I stood in the driveway and watched the tow truck take it away. When it was out of sight, I stuffed the bandanna in my pocket and I went inside and baked three loaves of bread and when they were done, I baked three more. Neither Momma nor Jack said a word about it and when dinner time came and I was still in the kitchen, they ordered a pizza.

The lime-green bandanna, probably still soiled with my father's sweat, got tucked away into a shoebox, along with the hands of the saint that I had salvaged from the fire and the ten-dollar bill I had stolen from Daniel's wallet. I wanted there to be other things in this box. I wanted there to be the crystal that Norther had given me, a dried flower from Elaine's rubber boot display, the pictures that I didn't steal from Daniel's wallet, pictures that I would have valued more now than that ten-dollar bill. But I was a child then. I knew we needed money and I knew that Daniel was responsible for the fire and that he had betrayed my mother and that none of this would have happened if not for Topaz and I thought that we were homeless.

When I was seventeen, Jack had skylights put in my room for better painting light and he bought and had installed for Momma a claw-foot tub and for Roo, who had just turned eleven, he threw a party at a fancy amusement park. Jack's practice was doing very well.

It was the same year that Paw-Paw died. He was buried next to Uncle Jimmie and this time I got to feel for myself the cold metal chairs and see Gramma hold another folded triangle of flag in her lap. Once home, she tucked it into the closet on top of Jimmie's flag.

The house was filled with well-meaning neighbors and friends who had brought baked hams and green Jell-O salads that jiggled full of nuts and tiny marshmallows. It was easy for me to sneak away to Jimmie's room and to once again sit on the plaid bedspread with, this time, two flags in my lap. I wanted to remember whose was whose, to be able to tell them apart in the future, and I made a small ink mark on a white stripe of Jimmie's flag.

Nothing had changed in this room. The aftershave bottles, Cynthia's picture, the dark plaid curtains still drawn. While Gramma was alive, nothing would change. When I left, I closed the door with a click and I went outside to Paw-Paw's tool shed and I claimed his electric hedgers for my own. The boxwood bushes had not been clipped in years and they grew large and unruly in front of the house.

In 1986, I was accepted into the North Carolina School of the Arts. Jack warned me against getting a degree in art, saying that it was impractical. "What else would she get a degree in?" my mother asked him and he nodded, knowing that I wasn't suited for anything except what I had been doing all my life.

In college, I had two shows that were made up exclusively of my paintings, one of my earlier, more abstract stuff and the other of what I had evolved to, landscapes and old abandoned buildings, houses with histories that I could only speculate about, but never know. Drawing them was owning them or, at the very least, getting the pleasure of their company for a while.

The countryside surrounding Winston-Salem was full of abandoned buildings and every weekend found me driving down dirt roads looking for the tell-tale large oak trees that were usually the sign of an old yard. I started dating a gardener and he would come with me sometimes, but when he started digging up the daffodils and bushes that had been left behind, I refused to bring him along anymore. When I told him why, he called me a crazy fucking artist and then he broke up with me. The garden that he had planted for me outside my front door withered and died and finally grew full of weeds. It had once been tame, but now it grew as wild as the places I sought out to paint.

I went to the School of the Arts for two years before I dropped out. It was the summer of 1988. I had been hired by a woman who had seen my boxwood playhouse to make one for her child and, through word of mouth, my business was launched. I told Jack and Momma that I needed a year off, that I was making too much money to quit the boxwood playhouse business and return to school. Jack said that I didn't know what making money was and, compared to the salary of a lawyer, I know he's right. But I like what I do. It is not a bad life. I pay my rent, keep up the maintenance on my car, keep myself fed, and I can still find time for painting and drawing. I like it better than school and my boxwood playhouses have been pictured in the paper a couple of times and last year I talked to Roo's class in Richmond on career day.

I've been out of school for a year now and maybe eventually I'll go back. Jack says I need to and that it won't get any easier the older I get and that I can't go on making boxwood playhouses for rich people's kids. Momma says that I should listen to Jack, because, if not for Jack, I might not have been able to go to college at all. She told me, if not for Jack, we might still be living in Gramma's house or maybe in a house like Two Moons, a house with dirt-cheap rent and no plumbing that sat at the end of a long and slimy driveway.

Three weeks ago Gramma died. She was buried in between Paw-Paw and Jimmie. The trees surrounding the graveyard were brilliant with fall colors and one breeze after another came sweeping through the service, knocking down leaves in a clattering shower.

Jack and Roo left for Richmond immediately following the funeral, but Momma and I stayed behind for a week, sifting through the house, deciding what to keep and what to turn over to the auctioneer. I took with me Jimmie's and Paw-Paw's flags and the picture of Jimmie that was still taped to my mother's mirror. Momma did not seem to want anything.

"I just want to sell this place," she told me one night, sitting at the kitchen table over a bucket of Kentucky Fried Chicken. "I just want to leave and never come back."

"But your family's buried here," I said.

"Do me a favor, Cedar. When I die, have me cremated. It's cheaper and neater. I hate caskets."

"Okay," I said. "Do you want to be scattered or kept in a jar?"

"Scattered," she told me. "But I don't know where."

That night, I woke up to Momma crawling into Jimmie's single bed with me. "Scatter my ashes at Two Moons," she whispered. "That's where I want to be."

"We can go there," I told her. "You don't have to catch your plane. You can ride with me. We can go back and visit Two Moons."

"I couldn't," she said.

"Why not? Jack can handle it without you and you know he'd understand."

"I can't go back there."

Momma caught her plane the next day. At the airport, she hugged me and said, "Go back for me. Bring me something."

It was not easy to find. The Haw River and the 15-501 bridge were there, like always, but I must have spent an hour turning off the wrong roads and then I must have spent another thirty minutes passing by the driveway before I finally recognized it. It was the dented blue mailbox that gave it away. The trouble was that I had been looking for it to be on its old concrete-block post and it was lying in the ditch, where I finally caught sight of its color. When I stopped the car and looked more closely through the brush, I could see Elaine's rubber boot, still filled with dried and ancient flowers and above it, the old sign that said, "Welcome to Two Moons."

I got out and fought my way through the tangle of weeds and blackberry bushes to the sign. When I grabbed hold of it and yanked, it came off into my hands in two wet and rotting pieces. My left hand held Daniel's evergreen tree with the overlapping quarter moons and the words, "Welcome to Two Moons." My right hand held, "Inexperienced Drivers Park and Walk." I sat on the rock that Daniel had hidden my father's mail under and I fitted the sign's jagged edges back together. They fell apart in my lap. I looked towards the road and remembered sitting here with Norther, waiting for the school bus. I remembered the streamers that Elaine had decorated the mailbox with on our very first day of school. I got up and I grabbed Elaine's flowers out of the boot and I tossed them and the sign into the back of my car.

I had no idea what to expect from the driveway. I had never driven it, but I had gained experience negotiating washed-out dirt roads while driving outside of Winston-Salem, looking for places to sketch and paint. I gunned the motor and headed up. The driveway was worse than ever. I straddled gullies and I wrapped around the curves and I fishtailed through the big puddles and I arrived, the yard suddenly opening up to me like an animal that had not been fed. It loomed wild and overgrown and lonely. The house was a black knot on top of the hill. To the left were the barns and to the right, ivy had crept over the rocks of my placenta grave. I had two hours till sunset and I wasted every minute of it circling the house and visiting everything else. I don't know why. I don't think it was just Daniel's ghost I was afraid of, but everyone's. Woody's, Elaine's, Roxy's, Norther's, even Momma's and mine.

I visited the pottery barn first and I remembered the creak of the kickwheel as Woody sat hunkered over it, shaping a bowl with his muddy hands. I remembered our blankets spread on the floor and our boxes of donated clothes labeled with Momma's smudged charcoal print. There was an old car seat dragged in here now, and a small stack of sticks beside the woodstove and, lumping across the log walls next to the window, in orange spray paint, was a huge heart and the words, "Billy loves Belinda." In the window sill was a dirty champagne glass which I knew to be the one my mother tossed out of the outhouse while sitting on my father's lap. It was filled with dead wild flowers. I took it.

The next barn was Momma's basket barn and it was still stuffed with the hoard of blond baskets that she had woven during our last winter here. The baskets were filmy with thick, dusty cobwebs. I wondered why we didn't take them with us when we left. Momma had woven them to sell, but she had left them here. I wanted to take them all and I carted as many as I could to the car, filling the trunk and the back seat and the passenger seat, and yet still there were baskets left in the barn. I had chosen out three particularly beautiful ones and these I put in the car last. I had chosen one for Momma, one for Roo, and one for Jack.

I walked back down the hill to the picnic table beneath the oak tree. The paper lanterns from Roo's birthday party were gone, but pieces of string still remained dripping from the branches. I brushed the fallen leaves off and ran my hand along the wood of the table. It was greasy with mold now and no longer red in color, but mostly black and gray.

I visited the outhouse, past Elaine's flower gardens marked with circles of stones, past the vegetable garden marked with a row of old tomato stakes. Through the memory of my feet, I found the path, which was once well-worn and visible but now overgrown with weeds. Inside the outhouse, there was a roll of toilet paper sitting on the little bench. It was damp and shredded and surrounded by mice turds. Cobwebs draped across the seat. The Beatles pictures had been ripped down and only the corners remained stapled to the wall. I brushed the seat off and sat down and looked out into the yard towards the house. The orange extension cord still snaked through the trees and ended in a melted glob that dangled close to the porch.

I cut across the back yard to my placenta grave and I spent an hour pulling the ivy away. I don't know why. It was probably crawling back towards the rocks before I even left that day. But I pulled it back anyway and I sat beside the rocks and I wished that Momma was with me and I wondered where my father was and I thought about Topaz reaching behind her and grabbing one of these rocks while Daniel humped away on top of her. I remembered the next day, while Momma slept, I had come out here and I had replaced the one stone that had rolled away from the others.

The sun was setting and it was getting colder and colder and finally I walked up to the house and onto the back porch and I climbed into the rubble. Woody's hat had blown into a corner. There was melted tupperware which I picked up and then dropped again. And then I picked it up again. I pitched it beyond the porch, onto the lawn. I picked up a piece of yellow and blue pottery. Elaine's bread bowl. I pitched it towards the yard too. Woody's hat. A seared corn-cob pipe. The handle of my mother's honeysuckle pot. All of this went into the yard in a pile. I did not know what I would do with it all. Only that I would do something for Momma. A collage? A sculpture? I had to make something from the wreckage of Two Moons and I had to do it for Momma. Momma could never do it for herself.

One of my paintings was turned upside down and pinned under a sooty beam and I tugged at it until it came loose. A shred of material. Brown plaid, blackened with soot. My mother's robe. A slipper. Roxy's. I got down on my knees and started digging at the rubble with my hands, uncovering more and more of the people we had once been. The melted knob of the TV. The lid from a jar. The blade of Elaine's small hand shovel. With this I tore at the rubble. The deeper I went the more I found buried and the less exposed it was to weather.

The sun was setting pink and the trees were looking like black lace against the sky and still I dug. I found the old copy of *Winnie the Pooh*, fattened with moisture. The pages were sealed together and the cover was seared but I recognized it. It was getting dark now. I was alone in the woods, madly digging through a burnt-up house. A hinge. A doorknob. I could not stop. I felt close to something. I didn't know what. But it was dark. I could barely see. I put my hands into the rubble and sifted it through them, picking out hard kernels of charcoal, sifting, searching, sifting until something different lay in my hand. It did not crumble like charcoal. It was small and smooth. I could not see.

I felt my way out of the rubble and down the hill towards my car. The interior lights didn't work so I cut on the headlights and their beams shown eerily across what was left of Two Moons. An owl started hooting in the woods, so close that I could hear the chortle in its throat. The thing that I held in my hand was the bullet necklace that Jimmie had sent to Momma. It was just the brass casing, empty now, tarnished, blackened, but still with a shred of leather hanging off of it.

The last letter that Jimmie had written to my mother had never been read and had been destroyed in the fire, but the one before it had been read, many times, and its words blazed now in the ruins of Two Moons. It had been after a particularly bad battle and Jimmie had lost his best friend.

"I'll never forget the sound of the zipper on that body bag," he wrote. "I've heard it too much."

And then he signed off, not as he usually did, with a counting of the days he had left. Instead he signed off with the assurance that it was almost over. That he would soon be stateside. That he was a man who could return to the man that he had once been.

"I'll be home soon, Love Jimmie."